Hullabaloo in
the Guava Orchard

Hullabaloo in the Guava Orchard

KIRAN DESAI

VIKING
Penguin India

in
association
with

ff
faber and faber
LONDON · BOSTON

VIKING
Penguin Books India (P) Ltd., 210 Chiranjiv Tower, 43 Nehru Place, New Delhi 110 019, India
Penguin Books Ltd., 27 Wrights Lane, London W8 5TZ, UK
Penguin Books USA Inc., 375 Hudson Street, New York, NY 10014, USA
Penguin Books Australia Ltd., Ringwood, Victoria, Australia
Penguin Books Canada Ltd., 10 Alcorn Avenue, Suite 300, Toronto, Ontario M4V 3B2, Canada
Penguin Books (NZ) Ltd., 182-190 Wairau Road, Auckland 10, New Zealand

First published by Faber and Faber Limited 1998
First published in India in Viking by Penguin Books India (P) Ltd. 1998
Published in association with Faber and Faber Limited

The sayings on p. 175 are taken from Bhargava's *Standard Illustrated Dictionary of the Hindi Language*, compiled by R.C. Pathak, BA, LT, 5th ed., Bhargava Book Depot, Chowk, Varanasi, 1989

Kiran Desai is hereby identified as author of this work in accordance with Section 77 of the Copyright, Designs and Patents Act 1988

Printed and bound in India by Ajanta Offset and Packagings Ltd., New Delhi

For my family
with love

That summer the heat had enveloped the whole of Shahkot in a murky yellow haze. The clutter of rooftops and washing lines that usually stretched all the way to the foothills at the horizon grew blurred and merged with the dust-filled sky.

'*Problems have been located in the cumulus that have become overly heated,*' read Mr Chawla from the newspaper. '*It is all a result of volcanic ash thrown up in the latest spurt of activity in Tierra del Fuego.*'

And a little later he reported to whomever might be listening: '*The problem lies in the currents off the West African coastline and the unexplained molecular movement observed in the polar ice-caps.*'

And: '*Iraq attempts to steal monsoon by deliberately creating low pressure over desert provinces and deflecting winds from India.*'

And even: '*Hungarian musician offers to draw rain clouds from Europe to India via the music of his flute.*'

'Why can't they think of serious solutions?' asked Mr Chawla. 'It is too hot to fool about with Hungarian musicians.'

Shahkot boasted some of the highest temperatures in the country and here there were dozens of monsoon-inducing proposals. Mr Chawla himself submitted a proposal to the forestry department for the cutting and growing of vegetation in elaborate patterns; the army proposed the scattering and driving of clouds by jet planes flying in a special geometric formation; the police a frog wedding to be performed by temple priests. Vermaji of the university invented a giant fan which he hoped would attract the southern monsoon clouds by creating a wind tunnel moving north towards the Himalayas, and he petitioned the Electricity Supply Board for enough power to test it. Amateur scientists from Mr Barnala of Tailor Gully to Miss Raina from the Sainik Farms area attended trade fairs where they displayed instruments that emitted magnetic rays and loud buzzing sounds. Everyone in the town was worried. The mercury in the police station thermometer exceeded the gradations Kapoor & Sons Happy Weather Company had seen fit to establish, leaping beyond memory and imagination, and outdoing the predictions of even Mr Chawla's mother, Ammaji, who liked to think she knew exactly what the future would bring.

It was a summer that sent the dizzy pulse of fever into the sky, in which even rules and laws that usually stood straight and purposeful grew limp, like plants exposed to the afternoon sun, and weak. The heat softened and spread the roads into sticky pools of pitch and melted the grease in the Brigadier's moustache so that it drooped and uncurled, casting shadows on his fine, crisp presence. It burned the Malhotra's daughter far too dark for a decent marriage and caused the water, if it came at all, to spurt, scalding, from the taps. The bees flew drunk on nectar that had turned alcoholic; the policemen slept all day in the banana grove; the local judge bribed an immigration official and left to join his brother in Copenhagen. Foreigners in their tour buses turned and went home, while Shahkotians argued for spots directly below their ceiling fans, leaving only for minutes if absolutely necessary and then hurrying back. In the marketplace, they raided the shops for palm leaf fans and bought grey blocks of ice that smoked like small fires. They rested their heads against the coolness of melons before cutting into them, held glasses against cheeks and foreheads between sips, fanned themselves at the stove with bunches of spinach before letting go reluctantly, for the sake of the evening meal.

The weeks passed, but the monsoon did not arrive. And by the time it was September, they had given up hope.

It was this year that Sampath Chawla was born to his mother, Kulfi. She was twenty-one years old, newly married to Mr Chawla, and pregnant. By late September the heat and lack of rain had combined to produce terrible conditions of drought. She grew bigger as it got worse. It got to be so bad that famine-relief camps were set up by the Red Cross to the west of Shahkot. The supply planes flew right over the bazaar and Shahkotians, watching with their heads tilted back, wondered why they didn't stop for them as well, for surely they were suffering quite enough to warrant the same attention and care being so assiduously delivered elsewhere. The ration shop was distributing rice and lentils in smaller and smaller portions all the time. There was no fruit to be found anywhere and hardly any vegetables. Prices had risen so high, nobody would buy the scraggy chickens sitting in cages outside the meat shop. Finally the poor butcher had to eat them himself, and after the last one, he was forced to turn vegetarian like the rest of the town.

Kulfi, in these months, was so enormously large, she seemed to be claiming all the earth's energy for herself, sapping it dry, leaving it withered, shrivelled and yellow.

People stopped short in amazement as she walked down the street. How big she was! They forgot their dealings in the almost empty marketplace. They teetered on their bicycles as they looked around for just another sight of that stomach extending improbably before her like a huge growth upon a slender tree. Her eyes were so dark, so sooty and vehement, though, these people who turned their heads to stare turned quickly away again, ill at ease for some reason and unsettled. Not noticing them, she passed by as if they weren't there at all. On her face, about her mouth and in the set of her chin was an expression intent and determined but yet far away and distant, as if all her thoughts were concentrated upon a point invisible to everybody but herself. She walked through Shahkot like this, as distracted as this, as strange as this.

'What do you expect?' asked Ammaji, her mother-in-law, making excuses when curious neighbours asked about Kulfi's state of mind. 'What do you expect from a woman with a baby in her belly like a little fish?'

But Kulfi was not thinking of the baby in her belly like a little fish. She was thinking of fish themselves. Of fish in many forms. Of fish big enough and good enough to feed the hunger that had overtaken her in the past months like a wave. She thought of fish curries and fish kebabs. Of pomfret, bekti, ruhi. Of shoals of whiskered shrimp. Of chewy mussels. She thought of food abundant in all its many incarnations. Of fenugreek and camel milk, yam and corn. Mangoes and coconuts and custard apples. Mushrooms sprouting like umbrellas in the monsoon season. Nuts, wrinkled in their shells, brown-skinned, milky-fleshed.

The house was small for her big desire. She walked from the tiny blue bedroom to the kitchen thick with the smell of kerosene, around the table and chairs, up and down the balcony, down the stairs past the rooms of neighbours who shook their heads over her, then around the jamun tree in the middle of the courtyard.

'Oh dear, what is going to become of this woman?' said Lakshmiji, the Raipurs, the Bengali teacher, and all of the others when they looked out of their windows, when they gossiped at the tea stall or sat in each other's houses eating peanuts together. 'There was always something odd about her,' they said. 'You could tell this from the minute she entered Shahkot.'

Meal after meal of just rice and lentils could not begin to satisfy the hunger that grew inside Kulfi; she bribed the vegetable sellers and the fruit sellers and the butcher with squares of silk, with embroidery, a satin petticoat, an earring set in gold, a silver nutcracker, bits of her dowry that had not yet been pawned. She bribed them until they had nothing left to give her anyway. By then, her hunger was so fierce, it was like a big, prowling animal. In her mind, aubergines grew large and purple and crisp, and then, in a pan, turned tender and melting. Ladyfingers were flavoured with tamarind and coriander. Chicken was stewed with cloves and cardamom. She thought of chopping and bubbling, of frying, slicing, stirring, grating.

'What on earth is she doing?' shouted Mr Chawla as he watched his wife disappear down the road to the marketplace again and again, as he surveyed the emptying cupboards in the house, the missing items, the gaps on the shelves. 'What have you married me to, Amma?' he demanded ferociously of his mother, who looked worried as well. However, since she was responsible for the marriage, she put her worry as far from herself as possible, clucked her tongue and said soothingly: 'She is at a very delicate stage. Wait a little and maybe she will come out of it.'

'Come out of it.' He snorted. 'She is not going to come out of it. And if the baby takes after her, we are really in for trouble.'

Oddness, like aches and pains, fits of tears and lethargy, always made him uneasy and he had a fear of these uncontrollable, messy puddles of life, the sticky humanness of things. He intended to keep his own involvement with such matters to the minimum, making instead firm progress in the direction of cleanliness and order. He went to the public library to look for books about babies and waited in line outside the Mission School to enrol the baby well in advance, for he knew how long the waiting lists were. He collected vitamins and tonics from the government clinic.

'You must take care to boil your drinking water for twenty minutes.' He followed Kulfi about the house reading aloud from his library book as she ignored him. He held one of his fingers up in the air. Despite his young age and slight build, he felt a powerful claim to authority. 'You must sit down and rest after any exercise,' he advised. And: 'You must stand up and exercise regularly and diligently.' And: 'Don't eat raw fruit any more.' And: 'Don't sing songs and tire yourself out. Don't drink tea on an empty stomach. Keep yourself extra clean. Wash your hair, take a nap, put your legs up in the air and do bicycling exercises.' He wiped the sweat from his forehead with a handkerchief and continued following his wife, even though it was clear she had no interest whatsoever in what he was saying.

Ammaji had her own ideas. She had her own ideas of how a woman's pregnancy should be managed. She fussed with pillows and herbs, with hairbrushes and bottles of strong-scented oil for massages. 'Sing songs to improve the baby's mood,' she advised. 'Go to the temple. Say the right prayers. Make sure the baby is healthy. Make sure the planetary configurations are good. Make sure you have no lice. Make sure you smell nice, and the baby will smell nice too.'

Everywhere there was the feeling of breath being drawn in and held, as if it wouldn't be let free again until the baby was born and it could be released – released happy and full of relief if the baby was a boy; released full of disappointment and resentment if it wasn't.

In Kulfi's stomach Sampath was at first quiet, as if he weren't there at all. Then, as if excited, he grew bolder and more full of life, until he kicked and turned and even leapt. Kulfi paced up and down, up and down, with her hands upon her belly and thought she might soon begin to scream, and that, whether she wanted to or not, she might continue to scream all the way up until the birth and maybe even after. Her stomach grew larger, her dreams of eating more extravagant. The house seemed to shrink. All about her the summer stretched white-hot into an infinite distance. Finally, in desperation for another landscape, she found a box of old crayons in the back of a cupboard and, with a feeling bordering on hysteria, she began to draw on the dirty, stained walls of the house. She drew around the pictures of babies Ammaji had put up. Babies eating porridge, posing with dolls and fluffy yellow chicks, attempting somersaults. Babies fat and fair and male that Ammaji hoped would somehow, through some mysterious osmotic process, influence the formation of her grandchild. Kulfi drew around these pictures and sometimes over them. She drew a pond, dark but leaping with colourful fish. A field of bright pineapples and pale, dangling snake-gourd. Big lumbering jackfruit in a jackfruit tree and a scratching bunch of chickens. As her husband and mother-in-law retreated in horror, not daring to upset her or the baby still inside her, she drew a parade of cooks beheading goats.

Others running to a marketplace overflowing with things to bargain over. Some standing over steaming pots with ladles or pounding whole spices on a grinding stone. She drew creepers and vines that climbed in at the window and spilled a wilderness of leaves upon the walls. She began to draw fruit she did not know; spices yet to be discovered in hidden pods or sequestered in the heart of unknown flowers. She drew dishes that she had never eaten: a black buck suspended over a fire with a row of ingredients destined to transform it into magnificence; a peacock cavorting among cloves of garlic; a boar entangled in a jungle of papaya trees. Onions grew large beneath her feet; creepers burst from the floorboards; fish swam beneath the doors.

In the next room was the sound of Mr Chawla pacing up and down. 'What have we got ourselves into?' The sound of Ammaji whispering: 'Just wait a little, beta, wait and see.' Outside, in the barren sky, the drone of the Red Cross planes.

When there was almost no space left to draw on any more, when the walls, floor and ceiling were full, packed tight to the point of bursting, Sampath was born. And he was born in such remarkable circumstances, they were remembered for ever afterwards by the people of Shahkot.

One day, as Kulfi was at the bedroom window looking at the street, prepared to sit through another seemingly endless stretch of time until Ammaji finally cooked and served her dinner, all of a sudden a shadow fell across the sun and magically, as quickly as a winter's day tumbles into smoky evening and then night, the white-lit afternoon deepened into the colour of old parchment as the sky darkened. Curtains billowed white out of every window. Bits of news-

-8-

paper and old plastic bags turned cartwheels in the indigo streets. The air thinned and stirred in a breeze that brought goose bumps out upon her arms. 'Look!' Kulfi shouted. 'Here comes the rain!'

She could hear the sound of cheering from the bazaar. And she watched the children in the streets leap like frogs, unable to keep still in their excitement. 'It's getting cold,' they shouted, and pretended to shake. 'It's going to rain.' They wrestled and tussled with each other in an exuberance of spirit, while the grown-ups hurried, in this shifting, shadowed light, to get to the market and back, to bring in washing, to carry in string cots. They raised their hands in greeting to each other: 'At last! The monsoon!' Who knew whether it came because of the giant fan, the wedding of frogs, the Pied Piper, because of mercurial powers or magician's marvels? And in the end, who cared? The rain had come to Shahkot. The monsoon was in town. Kulfi watched with unbelieving elation as the approaching smell of rain spiked the air like a flower, as the clouds shifted in from the east, reached the trees at the town's edge and moved in.

In the Chawla household, Mr Chawla bustled about with plastic sheeting, while Ammaji placed buckets outside to catch the rainwater and brought out candles and kerosene lanterns in preparation for the inevitable breakdown of electricity. They paused, though, to test the growing strength of the wind against their cheeks; looked up to check the progress of the clouds. When they were finally prepared for the downpour, they watched from the windows like Kulfi and the rest of Shahkot's residents, leaning from balconies and verandas, from beneath the flaps of scooter rickshaws; the entire town, with anxious, upturned eyes, until an especially strong gust sent the leaves flying like birds before gunshot and brought the first drops of water to sound loud against the parched earth.

Kulfi watched the rain. It came down fast and then faster yet. It filled up every bit of sky. It was like no other sound on earth and nothing that was ever suggested by the thin trickles from Shahkot taps. It came down black with dust from the sky and dirt on the trees, and then clear. But always louder. She stretched out her hands to feel the weight of the drops on her flat palms and then put her face out too, holding it, luminous, pale, in this town enclosed within the dark heart of the monsoon.

As she did so, she felt Sampath kick inside her stomach. Her heart jumped in rhythm. He kicked harder and harder. The jamun tree in the courtyard thrashed and creaked. The rain streamed down Kulfi's hair and washed over her face. Her husband shouted: 'Get away from the open window.' She paid no attention. He wrapped her in a square of plastic, but she shrugged it off. The rain descended in great sweeping sheets.

The neighbours withdrew in quick, sharp movements, slammed their windows, barred their doors, but Kulfi stretched out farther still, farther and farther until the rain took up all the space inside her head. It seized her brain, massaged and incorporated her into the watery sounds, until she felt that she herself might turn to storm and disappear in this blowing, this growling, this lightning flutter quick as a moth's wing. If she would only let go of the metal window frame, she could take all those tedious days of summer and crash them to the ground, transform them into water and wind and pounding.

She felt her muscles contract as a clap of thunder echoed about her. Again, the thunder roared. Kulfi, soaking wet, opened her mouth wide and roared back. Below her, the ground had disappeared. Ponds formed, joined to make lakes and ran down streets to make rivers. Rivers took the place of roads.

A mere two hours later, Mr Chawla and Ammaji running back and forth with cloths and hot water, the storm still raging, rain pouring through windows that would not stay closed and flooding in beneath the doors, Sampath was born. As his face, with a brown birthmark upon one cheek, appeared to the cheers of his family, there was a roaring overhead that almost split their eardrums, followed by a vast crash in the street outside.

'What was that?' said Mr Chawla nervously, as the ground shuddered. Could it be that his son's birth had coincided with the end of the world? Leaving Kulfi and the new baby, he and Ammaji ran to the window to investigate, and discovered that far from being the end of things it was more like the beginning.

Caught in their old jamun tree, they saw a crate of Red Cross supplies that had been dropped by a Swedish relief plane befuddled by the storm in a move that must surely have been planned by the gods. The departing plane rose high into the sky and vanished among the swirling clouds, unmoved apparently by the townspeople jumping and waving down below as they ran out despite the downpour to greet this unexpected largesse. Draped in the foliage of the ruined jamun, they discovered containers full of sugar and tea, of rehydration mixes, dried milk powder, raisins and digestive biscuits. There were unidentifiable powders in packages covered with pictures of smiling foreign women. There were nuts, sweets and baby-food tins galore. Filling their arms with their share of this booty, they ran up and down.

Climbing high into the tree, the street urchins tossed down what they found lodged in the broken branches. Mr

Chawla ran back and forth like a silly chicken, filling a shopping bag with supplies, while Ammaji alerted neighbours to the birth by shouting out of the window near Kulfi's bedside. Soon the house was full of well-wishers, chattering excitedly, not knowing whether to talk of the baby or the rain or the food. 'Wonderful,' they kept exclaiming, water dripping from their clothes to form pools about their feet. 'What a beautiful baby . . . and can you believe the monsoon? Oh and the food! . . . What a baby!'

Only Kulfi was quiet. She looked at the tiny creature in her hands, a creature that looked as if he had come from another planet altogether, or had been discovered in the woods, like something alien and strange. The baby's eyes were closed and his fingers were tightly curled. His face was red and his skull pointed. She looked at his strangeness and felt a sense of peace and comfort descend upon her. Soon the storm would end and the world would grow silent and fragrant, the air weathered soft as the hour of sleep. Soon the winged ants would be flying and lizards would grow fat on dozens of multiplying insects. The water would turn muddy and soft. Doors would swell and it would be impossible to close them once opened, or to open them once closed. Fungus and mould would sprout green and voluptuous and armies of mushrooms would gather in the cupboard under the sink.

Attempting to include Kulfi in their high spirits, the neighbours assured her that her son was destined for greatness, that the world, large and mysterious beyond Shahkot, had taken notice of him. 'Look! Even people in Sweden have remembered to send a birthday present.' And: 'Let's name him Sampath,' they said. 'Good fortune.' For though he might not be very plump or very fair, he was triumphantly and indisputably male.

In great good humour, chewing on famine relief, they celebrated by the light of a roomful of candles, for the electricity had, of course, gone.

2

Twenty years later, in the very same house and in the very same room, Sampath Chawla, with spider-like legs and arms, thin and worried-looking, lay awake under a fan. It thrashed and swung above him, making as much noise as a gale, although Sampath could feel only the faintest tremor of an air current playing about his toes.

All around him, his family lay and snored: his father, mother, grandmother and his younger sister, Pinky, swathed in quantities of flowered organza. Rrrrr. Rrrrr. Phurrrr. Wheeeeee. Rrrrrrr. What a racket! Sampath listened to each hostile inhalation. Even in sleep, he thought, disgusted, his family showed themselves incapable of pleasant displays of consideration. Self-indulgent as always, they worked their way noisily through their dreams, keeping Sampath, meanwhile, awake and tossing. Even his mother, whom he loved most of all, had forgotten him in sleep.

He kicked a foot up into the air with impatience. 'Sshhhhh,' he said out loud, but it was a poor, sad sound and they took no notice. Wheeeeeeeee. Rrrrr. Rrrrrr. It was too bad they were not rich enough for everyone to have their own room and their own fan. However, Sampath decided, for his own sake, it would be best to suppress his irritation. His family might be unable to respect the holy silence with which sleep should be imbued, but he would not lose his temper.

Making a new effort and a new start, he moved his body around so his head occupied the place where his feet had been. The puny bit of breeze picked up a strand of his hair and dangled it over his face so it tickled like a fly. He grabbed at it, pulled it out, scratched his face and composed himself again.

The fan squeaked. He thought it might fall on top of him, smashing his face as flat as a child's drawing. This thought became more and more persistent. The electrician, after all, had just been cleaning it, and it was well known in the whole of Shahkot how shamefully bad Bunty Chopra was at his job.

Sampath got up from under this dangerous appliance and lay on the floor, spreading his arms and legs and fingers as far apart as he could, so that not a single part of his sweaty, uncomfortable body would touch another. He lay flat like that and opened his mouth wide to facilitate the easy intake of air and, he hoped, the quick arrival of dreams. As soon as he had thus arranged himself, however, the power failed and the fan slowed to a standstill. Instead of dissipating into some blissful, cloudy realm, Sampath's concentration sharpened like a knife at all the places where his bones pressed against the hard floor. Once again, despite himself, he became conscious of the snores of his family who loomed alarmingly above him now he was on the ground, their hips rising like mountains far too high to climb.

How did they expect him to rest as they roared and vibrated like giants? As they sent their snores all the way to the top of the ceiling? Back and forth so the disturbing qualities of each sound accumulated and weighed on Sampath like a grinding stone? The room was hot and stuffy. His body felt heavy and dull. He knew, in a flash, that it might never be possible for him to move again. He was drowning; he would sink like a stone to a place as deep and dark as the sea floor. Making a heroic effort, propelled by a terrible feeling of panic, Sampath brought all the strength of his will together. In a crucial show of determination, unwitnessed by anyone, he rose, ran into the living room and burst through the door that led to the roof.

Upstairs, however, it was as hot as in the room below. The moon was pale and mildew-like, just a lifeless smudge against the night. Not one of the streetlights worked, and they wouldn't work, everyone knew, until the next local election. Then there would be a flurry of excitement, with five- and ten-point plans for the improvement of electricity supplies, and enough modern technology, they always promised, to send Shahkot and its residents bounding into the twenty-first century. Sampath walked up and down, the pale glow of his white pyjama kurta the only moving thing in this night so still, it seemed to be moulding itself perfectly against his body, so he knew it would be impossible to shake off; that there it would be, clinging to him even if he jumped or beat around him with a stick.

Up and down, back and forth. He walked to calm himself, as you would walk with a baby who cries and cries and cannot sleep. Above, there weren't any stars, only the lights now and then of planes, flying on their way to who knows where. To Calcutta? Madras? Madurai? To England or America? It was a terrible thing to be awake while some people flew, carrying the world over his head, and others slept, claiming it from under his feet. He was grateful, though, for the feel, rough and sandy, of the bricks beneath him, the uneven surfaces and the thin-ridged crisscross of lines. For the cool smoothness, now and then, of a fallen leaf. He picked them up one by one and held them against his lips to imitate the dull brrrrrr of a cricket; rolled them against his cheek and in his hot, sticky fingers, until they too became damp and warm. He sampled some ginger pickle from a jar set out to mature on the roof along with a whole row of mango, lime and pumpkin pickle jars. As the night wore on, he sampled a bit from every jar so as to decide on which kind, if any, he liked best. And by and by, between mouthfuls, without even knowing it, he started to sing: 'Sooner or later,' he sang softly, 'there will come a magic hour, when I spot a princess from the kingdom of Cooch Behar.'

A passing car sent its searchlight-glare crazy and liquid over the sides of the buildings and into the trees, revealing not the colours, the daylight solidity of things, but a world of dark gaps cut from an empty skin of light.

'When my mouth I'll open, I'll think of nothing to say, and this lady so fine and beautiful will continue on her way. Goodbye, my princess of Cooch Behar, may we meet again –'

The sound of his small voice, so bravely singing, cheered him up a little.

By the time the night watchman cycled past on his way home from the wealthy neighbourhood where he worked, Sampath was shaky on his feet from lack of sleep. Phee . . . pheee . . . phee – the watchman blew his whistle as if in a nasty attempt to awaken all those who might still be sleeping.

Sampath watched as the shadows retreated, as Shahkot was offered up once again, whole and intact, with its over-flowing rubbish heaps and its maze of streets. Bit by bit he saw the jumble of wires spilling out at the top of the electricity pole and the dirty, stained walls of the houses that rose high all about him, with their complications of rooftops and verandas; their clutter of television aerials, washing lines and courtyards filled with bicycles and raggedy plants and all the paraphernalia of loud and large families. The municipal water supply was turned on. From every kitchen and bathroom in Shahkot there was the sound of water pumps, thin streams of water dribbling into the first in a long line of buckets and pots and pans waiting to be filled. Sampath's father appeared down below with his yoga mat. Women emerged from different houses, converging in their walk to the Mother Dairy booth, and the priests in the temple at the end of the road launched into song, their voices richer and stronger than Sampath's, their hymns rising, undulating, soaring over the rooftops.

Sampath wondered if the cloudiness in his mind could be driven away with strong morning tea, with a good brushing of his teeth; if the emptiness in his belly could ever be filled. Descending the steps back into the house, he met Ammaji leaving with her milk pail, her white sari in messy folds about her. She looked like a pale sea creature washed on to the shore, marked by the tides, crumpled and creased.

Ammaji looked at her grandson's tired eyes. 'Didn't you sleep?' she asked. 'How will you last the day?' She pinched his cheek with tender reproach.

3

In the courtyard down below, Mr Chawla began his morning exercises. Determined to start the day in a purposeful manner, according to schedule and habit, he spat out the last remnants of sleep and inertia in a perfectly aimed rainbow spray of spittle. He stood in a patch of sunlight where the shadows cast by the jamun tree could not reach him. Still, at the spot where the Red Cross crate had landed the night of his son's birth, there was a large gap that marred the tree's otherwise elegant proportions. Mr Chawla bent forwards to touch his toes, then backwards to form a perfect arc, one taut and tight enough to catapult himself into the sky.

'Ommmmm.' He let his voice fly in triumph over the rooftops. 'Ommmmmmm,' he roared, teeth gleaming in the morning rays. 'Ommmmm.' He informed the world that he, Mr R. K. Chawla (B.A., Pass), head clerk at the Reserve Bank of Shahkot, was ready for a new day. The air vibrated as if shot through by arrows. He was forty years old, hale and hearty. And if he was balding a little and had a small belly . . . well, he liked this look; it added importance to his words and inspired respect. He stepped out into the world firm-footed and sure, putting to shame the sorry young men who drooped about the town, ignoring their responsibilities. Slapping his chest and swinging his arms, he jogged up and down around the courtyard.

Later, as he oiled himself with coconut oil in the small bathroom, he shouted from behind the closed door: 'The tooth powder is almost gone. You could buy some more from Diana Stores.' Or: 'Why don't you go and see if Lakshmiji's fever is better?' Or: 'The drain must be unblocked. Don't come complaining to me when we're overtaken by the world's largest cockroach population.'

He hoped to inspire his family to seek out a day as full of promise and activity as his own would be. When he took a bath, he crashed the metal buckets together loudly and poured water over himself in energetic mugfuls, flooding the entire bathroom so that miniature waves sloshed through the gap beneath the door. When he emerged, smooth-cheeked and fresh, redolent with Lifebuoy soap, he stirred the house into such a commotion the family thought they'd need the rest of the day to recover.

His shirt needed to be ironed. His shoes had been discovered dusty, dirty and unpolished. His socks upset him because they gathered in folds about his ankles instead of snapping with the satisfying sound of good elastic to a desirable mid-calf level. Ammaji and Pinky ran up and down trying to carry out his demands.

While trying to coordinate all the various activities needed to solve these problems, Mr Chawla read out bits from the newspaper as was his custom. 'What did I tell you?' he said, delighted. 'Another corrupt politician! Before we are properly out of one international scandal, we are in another. Our politicians are growing careless. They are opening more Swiss bank accounts than they have Gandhi caps to distract us with. Not one truthful politician in the whole country. Yes, our parliament is made of thieves, each one answerable to the prime minister, who is the biggest thief of them all. Look how well he's doing.

With each new photograph he is fatter than before.'

Kulfi, though, was not interested. She sat by the window, thinking of the deep-scented, deep-hearted world of peppercorn berries, of cinnamon bark, of the flowerbuds of cloves and cassia, and the saffron stigmas of the crocus. On the walls behind her were traces of the drawings she had made so many years ago, still visible from behind a thin layer of whitewash. By this time, it had been generally acknowledged that she was a little eccentric to say the least. Her hunger during first one pregnancy and then another had settled into a permanent obsession with food. As the years progressed, she grew more peculiar. Ignoring completely the hullabaloo created by her husband, she continued to stare out of the window while her daughter complained about the choice of news items being read aloud.

'Hoo,' said Pinky, flapping her towel in exasperation as she paused on the way to the bathroom. 'What is there to get so excited about? It is always the same old story. Each year the same scandal. Why don't you read something that will affect us? For example, the Cinema Monkey. Is there anything about the Cinema Monkey?'

'What monkey?' asked her father, bewildered.

'See, you are completely out of touch with local issues! For the past month he has been creating havoc outside the cinema, harassing ladies, pulling at their saris until they drop their peanut cones. And all those boys from the university – they are going especially to the cinema, not to see any movies, but just to stand outside and watch the girls getting their clothes pulled off! Haw-ji-haw, I am too scared to go any more.'

Her father snorted.

'Why don't you take Sampath with you?' said Ammaji, trying to find Mr Chawla a good pair of socks while also sipping tea from a saucer. 'He can protect you.'

'Sampath!' said Pinky. 'What good will Sampath be! The monkey will probably choose me as the best person to target if Sampath is with me.'

'That's true,' Ammaji agreed and took another sip of tea. 'He is not very threatening. Poor Sampath,' she said. 'Look at him, sitting, sitting there as usual, with no raise in pay or promotion anywhere in sight.'

Mr Chawla looked over to where his son was slouched over the table, his breakfast a spreading untidiness of crumbs around his plate. Before him a fly, vibrating like a machine, circled lower and lower over the bowl of fruit that had been bought by his wife after much deliberation from the fruit stall. Careful as a pilot, it settled on the ripest plum in the dish. Imagine its delight in finding such a thing indoors; it ran up and down to gauge the size of its discovery, stopping only occasionally to rub its thin black hands together like a greedy businessman. Sampath lifted the ruddy globe of fruit to get a better view of its long-snouted face when, right by his nose, there was a whoosh of movement and Mr Chawla, taking notice of his son's distressing lack of initiative, brought down the rolled-up newspaper – Boom! – hard on the fly, leaving nothing but feeble legs waving above a dirty, jammy mess and a blur of iridescent wing.

'Where is your common sense these days?' said Mr Chawla. 'God only knows what cowdung heaps and garbage dumps these flies come from. Come on. Eat your breakfast.' He sat down at the table opposite him and put aside the paper. 'How is your work going?'

'All right,' mumbled Sampath.

The reply irritated Mr Chawla. 'All right!' he exclaimed, his eyebrows raised. 'All right? You don't sound very certain.

If things were going all right, you wouldn't be earning the same salary you were earning last year and the year before that, now would you?'

One by one, all Sampath's classmates had found employment. Even the ones with report cards that were just like his. Report cards with so many red Fs the letter seemed to have multiplied with abandon, run wild by the absence of competition from the rest of the alphabet. Only Sampath had been left idle, spending many blissful hours dreaming in the tea stalls and singing to himself in the public gardens, until at last Mr Chawla had found a suitable job for his son.

'What job?' all the curious and nosy people in Shahkot asked.

To these people, Mr Chawla said, 'He is in government service.'

Government service! People thought of afternoon siestas. Of tea boys running up and down with glasses of steaming milky tea all day long. They thought of free medicines at the dispensary and pensions. Of ration cards and telephones. Of gas connections that could be had so easily. They thought of how this was a country with many festivals and holidays. Of how the government offices closed for each one. They imagined a job where, even if your boss turned out to be unpleasant, there were always plenty of people to shout at, people whom you could shout at even louder than your boss had shouted at you. The sweeper or the messenger boy, for example. You could say: 'Where is your mind? Did it fall out on your way to work?' Or: 'Watch out or I'll give you a good kick that will send you from Shahkot all the way into the Bay of Bengal.' What pleasure there was to be had in a job like that! Really, it was a fine thing to have a son in the government. People thought of the Ministry of Finance. Of Industry. Of Forestry and Ladies' Welfare. Of Fisheries. Of Art and Culture. Of Transport.

Sampath, working at the back desk in the Shahkot post office, however, did not consider himself to be so terribly lucky.

Mr Chawla swallowed a whole clove of blood-cleansing garlic with a mouthful of water and a loud gulp. His son was so very annoying. He remembered how, as a young man himself, he had been so full of promise and efficiency. He had been smart, nimble and quick, the opposite of his son, who, now that the fly was dead, sat contemplating the mushrooming of milky clouds in his tea with a blank and hopeless expression on his face.

'A job,' he said to him, launching into one of the lectures he felt compelled to give Sampath every now and then, 'a job has two major sides to it. And it is of no significance if you are the prime minister or the sweeper boy, they are the same two points. First, the work itself. Put your best foot forward always. Even if it involves something a little extra, such as making railway bookings for your boss, don't complain. It is only a small thing.'

Ammaji came in from the kitchen where she was preparing the lunch boxes. Kulfi cooked only when inspiration overtook her; she left the humdrum cooking to Ammaji. 'Do you want plain parathas for your tiffin, or would you rather have parathas with radish?' asked Ammaji.

'I would like peacocks and pomegranates,' said Kulfi, so softly that nobody heard her.

Mr Chawla flapped his hand in impatience at his mother as he answered for both himself and Sampath. 'Radish,' he said and waved Ammaji away. 'When your boss speaks to you, stand up always – there is no harm in showing respect – and say: "I will see to it right now, sir." This brings us to the second major point.'

His mother came in again. 'I could make you aloo bhaji,' she said, 'if the parathas will not be enough.'

'Pheasants, peacocks, pomegranates,' said Kulfi.

But again nobody heard her and Mr Chawla addressed his mother: 'We are having an important discussion, and you are interrupting us with your talk of tiffin boxes! Do you want aloo bhaji, do you want radishes . . . here we are trying to talk about Sampath's career prospects.'

'But what am I talking about?' she protested. 'I am also talking about Sampath's career prospects. If he didn't eat properly, he would not even reach the office. He would fall into the gutter from hunger. Anyway, how can you sit all day and add up numbers when in your stomach there is a zero amount of food?' she asked triumphantly.

'Put whatever you want in the lunch boxes,' he shouted back at her, bad-tempered. 'What does it matter? Why don't you think of something else for a change? What do you care if the sky falls on your grandson's head so long as he has a gulab jamun in his mouth? No wonder the boy has turned out like this, spending his life at the bottom of a ladder.'

Sampath sat between them, looking as if he might just keel over.

'He is like this,' said Pinky, painting her nails in the morning sun that streamed through the window and surveying her hands with satisfaction. 'He is like this by nature. But he should buy new shoes from Bata. Looking like that, he will not get anywhere.'

'Oh, leave him alone,' said Ammaji. 'His stars are good. This is just a temporary phase. Give him a good head massage every day and the obstruction to his progress will go away.'

'Phoo!' Mr Chawla snorted. 'Progress! Ever since he was born, this boy has been progressing steadily in the wrong direction. Instead of trying to work his way upwards, he started on a downward climb and now he is almost as close to the bottom as he could ever be.'

'But the world is round,' said Ammaji, pleased by her own cleverness. 'Wait and see! Even if it appears he is going downhill, he will come up out on the other side. Yes, on top of the world. He is just taking the longer route.'

'He is not taking any route, I tell you. He has missed the route altogether. He is just sitting by the side playing with flies.' Mr Chawla turned back to Sampath, who had closed his eyes, imagining a long and peaceful sleep in a cool dark place. 'Come on,' his father urged him. 'Get ready for work. It's nine o'clock. Why are you still sitting here like a potato?' He twitched with impatience. 'What is the matter with this family? I am the only one with any sense of responsibility, any idea of the way things work in this world. If it wasn't for me, Sampath would be sitting in a special museum for people who are a cross between potatoes and human beings.' In the tone of a tour guide, he intoned: 'Watch how this peculiar vegetable spends its day.' And, to show just what he thought of the way this peculiar vegetable spent its day, he picked up his lunch box and marched, each footstep firm and loud, down the stairs on his way to work.

'Pheasants, peacocks, pomegranates, potatoes . . . poor Sampath,' murmured Kulfi to herself.

4

The post office, like so many government buildings, was painted yellow. Over the years, it had faded to match perfectly the haze of dust that enveloped Sampath each time he bicycled in to work. He took a short cut that led down the main bazaar road, through the hospital grounds and then under the barbed-wire fence that had been erected about the post office compound to establish it as a place sacred to official order and duty. Naturally, the barbed-wire fence was not entirely intact, for the residents of Shahkot, never ones to respect such foolish efforts, had set to work as quickly as they could to dismantle this unfortunate obstruction. All about their own houses and in their gardens and courtyards, they discovered a sudden need for wire; and all through the day, while, say, picking an annoying wedge of betel nut from between their teeth, or lifting their feet into a friendly lap for a foot massage, inspiration for wire-use struck them. They had always wanted to scratch their names upon the bark of a certain tree or across the dome of a certain protected monument. A curtain needed hooks. A gate, some sort of latch. There was a plant that would not stand up straight. A goat that tried to eat the plant. A dog that tried to bite the goat. An urgent need for fencing close to home. Soon there were gaps all around, and wherever there weren't, one person or another had worked the wire up on stakes or trampled it down to allow for free movement about the town.

And so the post office stood in the middle of the hustle and bustle of Shahkot. Schoolchildren, beggars, potters and signboard painters. Cows and pigs and water buffaloes. Ikebana class teachers from the polytechnic. Mathematics tutors. Clerks from the asthma institute, and cooks. Lady doctors and the head of the mental asylum. Accountants. Hosiery products men. Umbrella repair men. A bread and egg man. A fish woman. Flies. A washerman barely visible beneath sheets and towels. An orange-robed sadhu smiling and bowing despite the heat. (Truly India is a land of miracles.) Scooters and rickshaws, trucks and cars. Everyone's mother, father, uncle, sister-in-law and fourth and fifth cousin-brother twice and thrice removed. And Sampath on his way to work with Pinky sitting on the back seat of the cycle, charting a zigzag line through it all as he sought out the promise of coolness alongside walls and under trees and awnings, for the morning sun was already hot. Dashing from one blue pool of shadow to another, he conducted an erratic path through the crowd, which responded with snorts and shouts, a vast blowing of horns and utter chaos.

'Stop!' Pinky thumped her brother. 'I am almost falling off the back here. Can't you even cycle straight?' They continued a bit farther. 'Let me off.' She hammered at him. 'This is too much. I am going to take the public bus instead. You are making me feel sick.'

He stopped and, glowering at him, Pinky straightened her fantastic outfit of sunset polyester and strode towards the bus stop. He watched her, resting for a minute as he drank a glass of ice-cold water from the water man's cart.

As the bus appeared around the bend, filled to bursting as usual, Pinky removed a hairpin from her hair so as to have a weapon against men who might misbehave on seeing such a pretty girl at close quarters. Throwing herself on to the overcrowded steps, hanging on, feet waving wildly in the air, she speared a man who was not only taking up too much room in her opinion, but had made the mistake of winking at her, unaware of whom he was up against. Sampath could hear him shouting in alarm as his voice carried out of the window of the bus and down the street.

Everyone on the bus shouted as well. Some in attempt to restore calm: 'But why are you making such a big fuss about a little thing like a wink?' Some in encouragement: 'Very good. Good for you. You show him.' Some disapproving and terse: 'There are some ladies who should be made to walk to work.' The bus disappeared in a billowing cloud of exhaust fumes.

When Sampath had finished coughing, he cycled on, taking a short cut that led through the hospital grounds, forgetting, as usual, to bend down low enough to pass under his own particular bit of raised wire when he reached the post office, so that a large tuft of hair was caught and wrenched from his head as he entered the compound. Perhaps it would later be claimed by the crows as a superior sort of nesting material. Was he, he wondered, an especially generous supporter of the increasing crow population of Shahkot? Would this make him prematurely bald? Or perhaps his hair, inspired by empty patches, would spring back thicker and more resilient than ever?

He addressed his questions to a passing cow. It looked back at him, sad-eyed, on the brink, it seemed, of big, wet tears. Before he had to suffer the silence of its response, Sampath answered for it hastily: 'Who can tell?' Then, propping his bicycle against a pillar, he made a who-can-tell? gesture in the air and hurried into the mail room.

Inside the post office, it was dark and grimy. Inexplicably, the only window was the little one through which they sold stamps and it was still firmly closed. Paper clips, forms and files lay all over a dirty grey floor and teetering towers of ancient ledgers and letters, black with dust, were stacked up to disappear into the discoloured mottled darkness above.

Sampath stood in the doorway, with his eyes shut tight so as to give them time for this transition from sun to shade. After all, he had not slept that night and he needed to be especially careful. He opened his lids slowly, releasing his pupils to discover the gloom, the air that resembled the shadows, the murkiness of pond water. This was summer: the landscape offering up only a few shabby colours, the senses mostly overwhelmed just by dark and light in harsh opposition.

'Oh, Sampath,' two voices exclaimed as he entered, evidently relieved to see it was him and not the head of the post office, and then continued with a conversation that was already in full swing. In a while Sampath could make out his fellow employees sitting in the dimness, discussing, with their legs up on each other's chairs, the very same monkey that Pinky had complained about that morning.

'It was very embarrassing,' said Miss Jyotsna. 'Before I knew it, that monkey had ripped my salwar and run away with my peanut cone. Now I have to get a new salwar made and you can just imagine what problems I am having with the tailor. I told him: "Either you do not know how to use a measuring tape or else overnight I have shrunk to half my size. How can I go walking around in a big tent? What looks I will get!" He said: "You will get looks, Aunty, because the salwar kameez suits you so well." "Don't call me Aunty," I told him. "Do you think I'm so old you can call me Aunty?" And look at what a mess he made with my petticoat . . .' She displayed from beneath her sari the ruffled flounce that had been so shoddily sewn.

Sampath was transfixed. Miss Jyotsna kicked her feet up in the air. (What red toenails! Jewel-like, beetle-like, beautiful red toenails!) His ears felt as if they'd been dusted with a light coating of paprika.

Mr Gupta, sharing none of Sampath's capacity for quiet observation, seized this chance for active involvement. 'Oh no!' He waggled his finger at her. 'Oh no. You should not wear that shade of green at any cost. Look at how it is clashing with your complexion.'

'Arre, Mr Gupta, what are you saying?' Miss Jyotsna asked with mock horror that made him laugh. (The teeth he displayed were shiny white, the kind of white that in a dusty and yellow country can be found only in certain protected places such as a mouth.)

'Don't you ever look in the mirror?' he teased. 'Look and you'll see that I am right. As always.' He winked.

'Will you be my fashion consultant for the wedding?' She laughed as well. 'Clearly you know much more than me. Doesn't he, Sampath?'

Flirtatiously, she poked Mr Gupta with a ruler so he giggled even more. 'What do you say? Will you tell me what to wear for the wedding?'

The wedding of the daughter of the head of the post office was to be held at the Badshah Gardens, adjoining his house, at the beginning of the wedding season. At that very moment they should have been engrossed in making arrangements with bands and kebab and rickshaw men, and doing the hundreds of other important tasks that must be undertaken at an occasion like this. For, of course, when it comes to a wedding, all official work should stop and the staff of any office whose boss's family is having a wedding must assist in making the appropriate arrangements. This is customary office protocol. They had all been given their own appointed tasks to carry out.

When this boss – the head of the postal and telegraphic services of Shahkot – arrived, they jumped to their feet in alarm.

'Good morning, sir.' Miss Jyotsna quickly smoothed down her sari.

'You will kindly begin the day's work,' said Mr D. P. S. 'Keep the post office closed. Make preparations for the flower garlands. Contact the sweetmeat vendor and the biryani cooks. Get the men to put up the tent. Make arrangements for chairs. You will kindly make reservations at the railway station. The receipts are to be placed on my table. You will kindly arrange it all.'

You would think he had learned his first words, and then all the words that followed, from some instruction booklet.

'You will kindly pull up your socks and begin,' he snapped.

Sampath's thoughts, all petticoats, toenails and monkeys, teetered. A wave of sleepiness overtook him. But, suddenly remembering the advice he had received earlier in the day, mimicking his father's tone of voice, he chirped 'Yes, sir. I will see to it right now, sir.' But once he began, the latter half of his sentence – the 'right now, sir' – amazed and shocked by the preceding words, grew shaky and trailed up thinly into the high ceiling of the room, where the fan revolved with an uneven flutter like an irregular heartbeat, cobwebs having been caught in the blades. They all turned to stare at him in surprise. Never had they heard him attempt such a sentence. It was most uncharacteristic. Realizing himself how odd he had sounded, his face burning, Sampath turned and scuttled off to his desk in the dark depths at the back of the post office.

'I am keeping my eye on you,' said his boss after him. 'Kindly no misbehaving.'

For a while, Sampath attempted half-heartedly to add together the costs of the wedding in an accounts ledger. Balanced on top of an old telephone directory to save himself from falling through the broken seat of his chair, he began to fill the file with numbers from the bills and receipts. But there were so many receipts and so many bills, and all so like each other, he became confused and had to start over again, and again, stacking them together and separating them, filing them backwards, mislaying them. He tried to follow the rows of numbers all the way to the bottom square marked 'Total', but no matter how hard he tried, how much he attempted to hone his attention to a single needle-sharp point, a pin upon which to spear number after number, his mind grew dizzier and dizzier, and he was forced to begin again until, afternoon rising in its giant push and swell, yawns blooming like buffers between him and the dusty pages, he turned his attention instead to the day's mail.

Mr D. P. S. had disappeared on an errand to the jewellers. Miss Jyotsna and Mr Gupta were teasing one another again. Sampath examined the postcards and letters that had just been brought in on the bus from Delhi for him to sort out into the order in which they were to be delivered. He turned them over, smelled them, looked at the stamps, studied the names, the strange-feathered words: Bombalapetty, Pudukkottai, Aurangabad, Tonk, Coimbatore, Koovappally, Piploo,

Thimpu, Kampala, Cairo, Albuquerque. He held them up against the light, the envelopes filled with promise, with the possibility of different worlds. He steamed them open over mugs of tea, or just prised them open, the humidity in the air having rendered the gum almost entirely ineffectual, and lazily, through the rest of the day, he perused their contents. Since he had started work in the post office, he had spent much of his time in this fashion. He had read of family feuds and love affairs, of marriages being arranged, of babies being born, of people dying and of ghosts returning, of farewells and home-comings. He had read of natural disasters, floods and earthquakes, of small trivial matters like the lack of shampoo. Of big cities and of villages much smaller than Shahkot. In some countries people took a bath only once a week and the women wore short dresses even when they were old. He picked up all sorts of interesting information. Once in a while, there were postcards sent from foreign countries to addresses in the posh localities of Shahkot, and Sampath sat for hours mulling over, say, a picture of a palm tree by a sea as blue as if it had been dyed with paint, or of a village belle from Switzerland in a tight-laced frock and two fat yellow plaits that resembled something good to eat. Switzerland was a cold country where there was not a speck of dirt. There in the afternoon heat of Shahkot, Sampath would imagine the cold and the clean so vividly, every hair on him would stand on end.

By evening, when it was discovered that he had finished none of the things he was supposed to have done, he was sent home with warning of dire consequences to follow; he was to come in before everybody else the next day and complete the work. How they tormented him! He had been having such a nice time, left to his own devices. And how was he supposed to concentrate? He had been unable to sleep that past night and also the night before, and no doubt he would also remain awake in the night to come.

It was curious how he thought of his sleepiness when he had to work, but miraculously forgot it when he came upon something that interested him. On his way home, he recalled a postcard he had seen of an ape with a very big and alarming red bottom.

5

A few months later, at the beginning of winter in Shahkot, when the nights were cool and the town was full of flowers, the wedding day of Mr D. P. S.'s daughter arrived. Soon after sunrise, as instructed by their boss, the entire post-office staff was on hand to perform such necessary tasks as hanging marigolds and chillies in the doorways, procuring strings of party lights for the trees, fetching young and tender goats for the biryani. Miss Jyotsna and Mr Gupta rose to the occasion with tremendous enthusiasm, shouting at the band members and the tent men for laziness, tasting kebabs for tenderness, meeting relatives at the train station, running with joy to the tailors and back again with bursting bags. This was not the time to let anyone down.

Sampath had been allotted the job of filling glasses with sherbet, of washing the glasses once they were emptied by the guests, and then filling them up again; it had been decided by group consensus that even Sampath could be counted on to manage this simple task. But, after all, it is very boring to sit filling and washing hundreds of glasses, especially after you yourself have drunk your fill. Sampath began to toss choice bits of food to the stray dogs that had gathered at the back of the wedding tent to see what they could scrounge from the feast. Then, when the cooks began to threaten – 'You stop that or we'll chop you up with the onions' – he decided to look around to determine the layout of the house. He opened doors and peered into cup-boards. He went through the contents of a drawer. But things were rather old and dusty. Nothing in Mr D. P. S.'s residence seemed terribly interesting until, at the end of the corridor, he came upon a room piled high with wed-ding finery in which the cousin-sisters had dressed each other and departed in a rush, leaving their belongings strewn higgledy-piggledy over the place. It was not the bride's dowry, which was under lock and key, of course, or the aunties' precious jewels, which had been locked up as well, but it was quite exciting all the same. The clothes for several days of celebration were scattered upon the floor, the beds and chairs.

He could see ruffles of peacock silk and tiny pleats of rosy satin; lengths of fabric and saris of every colour imag-inable. Fabric run through with threads of gold, scattered with sequins and bits of glass, with embroidered parrots and lotus flowers worked in silver. There were mango pat-terns in rich plum and luminous amber shades. There were dark velvets and pale milk-like pastels tinted with only the faintest suggestion of rose pink or pistachio. There were unbroken stretches of crisp white petticoats in waves about Sampath's feet.

He uncorked a bottle of rose-water and its fragrance escaped to mingle with the rich mutton biryani smells ris-ing from cauldrons outside. Sampath, whose sense of smell had been refined during years of paying close attention to the olfactory curiosities offered by the world, could also discern the scents of musk, of mothballs, marigolds and baby powder. Of sandalwood oil. Oh, scented world! He felt his heart grow light. He held the fabrics to his cheek, let their slippery weight fall from one hand to the other and slide over his arms. He swathed lengths of pink and green and turmeric yellow about himself until he looked like a box of sweets wrapped up for the Diwali season. In a box full of a cousin-sister's jewellery, he examined unusual iridescences: pearls hung upon stalks of silver; a stone lit with the brilliance of an eye; the delicacy of shell. He imagined the sun deep in the ear of a flower. He put a blue stone in his mouth, then took it out and rolled it, cool and round, up and down his arms. To his nose he attached a nose ring decorated like a chandelier with glassy, glinting drops. He wondered if he could be considered beautiful.

The room was quite dark, since he had closed both the window and the door so he might conduct his exploration undisturbed. In order to survey himself in all his finery, he lit a candle by the mirror and watched as he metamorphosed into a glorious bird, a magnificent insect. The mirror was mottled, slightly cloudy, speckled with age. He felt far away, lifted to another plane. Held within this frame, he could have been a photograph, or a painting, a character caught in a storybook. Distant, tinged with mystery, warm with the romance of it all, he felt a sudden sharp longing, a craving for an imagined world, for something he'd never known but felt deep within himself. The candle attracted his finger like a moth and he drew it back and forth through the yellow and blue flame.

He remembered how, not so long ago, the rest of the family asleep, he had spent dark hours over his books, always some examination to study for, some test or some long question to answer. He had wrapped a wet cloth around his head, hoping for coolness, but the sweat had trickled down his back like the quick run of a beetle, his fountain pen had grown slippery in his hands, ink smearing into monster tracks, blue and black across the page. How, even then, candle at his elbow, his finger had been distracted from the lines of print he hoped to follow all the way into memory; and like the moths that joined him, his finger too had sometimes been caught and singed.

The next day, he had known, he would leave blanks instead of answers to the questions chalked up on the blackboard – the ten most important political reforms introduced by King Asoka, the advantages and disadvantages of the caste system. They had retreated into the trembling scene before him, along with the soil and altitude requirements for a good crop of wheat; the stages of reproduction in the paramecium; and the proof, in an isosceles triangle, that an exterior angle is equal to the sum of the interior opposite angles.

He had watched as a piece of paper flared up in the night and crumpled. Collecting the dripping wax, soft and greasy, into a dozen balls of varying size, he had sliced through them with instruments from a geometry box; studied the wobbling globe of light cast through the belly of an empty glass; fingered the warped wood of the table. He had salvaged only odd words here and there from the pages in front of him. Slips of sentences. The thought of a river dark through pale country. The cool 'o's in Colombia, drawing the tongue over them as easily as water. He had traced the outlines of a map that showed the savannah grasslands of the world, run his finger over the backbones of the mountains in his atlas, down the veins of blue rivers. But he had forgotten the urgency of finishing the night's work, the importance of the next day's examination.

He had held the candle far enough away to lose its heat, yet close enough to keep its light around him. He remembered carrying it to the mirror. How, with its hot, eager breath in his face, the flame had illuminated into strangeness a chin and a cheek, or a hand, a nose, a mouth. He had watched his lips form words, any words: just 'hello' sometimes, or even 'mmmm'. The memory of them hanging in the air for a moment, then disappearing into the silence of the room, spreading to stillness like the ripples cast by a small pebble. Sometimes, though, he had made no sound at all, just worked his lips like a fish in the deep-shadowed light, mouthing the air like water.

Now he traced the outline of his face and drew in the fantastic costume. He smiled and bowed at his reflection as if he were his own honoured guest. The lizards on the wall watched him with severe eyes. He stuck out his tongue at them, felt suddenly and ridiculously happy. Perhaps he was made for a life hung with brocades, worked out in fine patterns of jewels. Perhaps he was made to wear silk slippers and, with a wave, demand the world's attention. Striking a pose, nose in the magical air, hand raised for a touch of drama, he sang, making up his own words to a popular tune: 'My suit is Japanese, tra-la-la, my lunch was Chinese, tra-la-la, but though I may roam, tra-la-la, don't worry, Mama and Papa, my heart belongs to home. Oh, my heart belongs to home.' He gyrated his hips in perfect circles.

Venturing out of the room to where the party had just begun, he was made brave by the smell of the biryani and kebabs; encouraged by the sparkle of elegant clothes and jewellery, by the clinking of plates and finger bowls, by the laughter of the arriving guests in the tent and the jostling sweets frying in clarified butter just outside. A red carpet stretched from the entrance of the marriage tent all the way to a fountain at the centre. Sampath cavorted up and down its length, tossing his nose ring, kicking his legs. Mr D. P. S. and his wife, plying their future son-in-law's family with drinks and snacks, greeted his advance upon them with stunned silence. Sampath felt as if his feet were far above the floor, as if, floating in some groundless state, he were missing the weight of his head, his stomach and all of his insides. 'Tomorrow it will be too late,' he sang, chandelier-style drops in his nose all aquiver. He waded into the fountain and jumped in the spray, splashing the grand ladies with water so they ran squealing in consternation. 'Meet me under the plantain tree,' he warbled, 'and there will be no more talk of heartache.'

And slowly, deliciously, feeling it was the right thing to do, Sampath began to disrobe. Horrified shrieks rose from his audience. However, in this flushed moment, he mistook them for cries of admiration. With a style particular to himself, one by one he let the saris and dupattas draped about him fall. He unwrapped the last glittering length of fabric, but still he felt he had not yet reached the dazzling pinnacle of his performance, the pinnacle he strove towards, that his whole being was in anticipation of. He could not let himself down and he began to unbutton his shirt. He tossed the garment into the air like a hero throwing away the rag with which he has cleaned the weapon that will kill his enemy. As the shrieks grew in volume and intensity, he lowered his hand to his pants. 'Stop him,' shouted Mr D. P. S., and several people rushed forwards. But Sampath climbed deftly on to the highest tier of the fountain and, in one swift movement, lowered both his trousers and his underpants. His back to the crowd, he stuck his brown behind up into the air and wiggled it wildly in an ecstatic appreciation of the evening's entertainment he himself had just provided.

'Haiiii. What did you do?' shouted the family when Sampath returned home, jobless, sober and soaked to the skin.

'Kindly remove yourself,' Mr D. P. S. had said to him, so

coldly Sampath's heart had frozen over. 'It is no longer necessary to report to work.'

But he hated his job anyway. He didn't want his job. He didn't want it, he couldn't do it and he didn't want another job. He would not be able to do that either. He felt defiant. But . . .

'What! You have lost your job!'

'Hai, hai, this boy is nothing but trouble and misfortune.'

'You are completely lacking in common sense.'

'Did you get water in your nose?'

'What are we going to do now?'

'You really took off your underpants?'

'The dye from the wet clothes has stained you blue. Quick. Soap yourself clean.'

'From tomorrow onwards, you had better start looking for a new job.'

'Wet hair leads to a cold in the head. A head massage with gingelly oil keeps the brain warm.'

'Go to the Office of Public Transport tomorrow morning and apply for a position.'

'Did you open your mouth in the fountain? That water is all recycled sewage water. You could have swallowed tiny worms.'

'Think of interview strategies.'

'If you go barefoot in dirty water all sorts of germs will enter your body through your toes. Put on some socks and shoes.'

'You are an absolute good-for-nothing. Go to the Bureau of Statistics tomorrow afternoon and see if they have any openings. Go to the hospital, to the convent, to the agricultural centre, to the electricity office . . . To the Anu Dairy Farm, to the Utterly Butterly Delicious Butter Factory.'

Mr Gupta and Miss Jyotsna came to offer their condolences.

'Arre, Sampathji, how could you do that?'

'Now you are really keema kebab.'

'Now you'll be on vacation for ever after . . .'

How they all went on and on! How they all talked and shouted.

Sampath felt as if they had conspired to build a net about him, what with all their yelling and screaming, to catch him and truss him up for ever. Their questions ate away at him. His head ached, and so did his heart. He felt dreadfully sorry for himself. 'What did I do?' he shouted. 'I didn't do a thing. Stop shouting at me. Stop talking. Keep quiet. Keep quiet. Keep quiet.' He went out on to the balcony and slammed the door behind him. But they continued. Even now he could hear them through the door. He climbed up on to the roof.

How he hated his life. It was a never-ending flow of misery. It was a prison he had been born into. The one time he had a little bit of fun, he was curtailed and punished. He was born unlucky, that's what it was. All about him the neighbourhood houses seemed to rise like a trap, a maze of staircases and walls with windows that opened only to look into one another.

He felt bitter at heart. Surely, he thought, his surroundings were detrimental to his mental health. The sky was a series of squares and rectangles between clothes lines and television aerials, balconies, flowerpots and water tanks. It looked like pieces from a jigsaw puzzle.

How would you approach this problem?

Strangely, for some odd reason, from way off in the distance, he remembered the taunting voice of Father Matthew Mathematics at the classroom board at the Mission School.

Show all steps leading to the end result for full marks.

In his mind the days, his work, his life and even his thoughts all whirled. The same days. The same place. The one road –

The post office at the end of his journey like a full stop.

He did not want another job.

He wanted open spaces.

And he wanted them in large swathes, in days that were clear stretches he could fill with as little as he wished. Here a person's experience of silence and space squeezed and warped into underground forms that were forced to hide, found in only a few places that Sampath could discover. In his small lapses from duty; between the eye and the print of a newspaper held by someone who never turned a page; in a woman who stared into the distance and past the blur of knitting needles in her fingers; behind muttered prayers; once in a long while in eyes that could look past everything to discover open spaces. But no, Sampath was to be allowed no peace whatsoever. He was found out and turned away from every refuge he sought.

'Hai, hai, what will become of that boy?'

'And it took a whole year to find that post-office job . . .'

Around him large pigeon families cooed and fussed in the flowerpots in an effort, it seemed, to enclose themselves in a world of woolly comfort. Sampath, suddenly angry, stamped his foot to scare them. They rose, only to settle again. Coo, fuss, coo, fuss.

From a window below, his mother's head appeared, sticking out. Apparently she too was in need of a little quiet after all the noise in the house. He watched as she leaned out, craning her neck to look into the shopping bag of someone returning from the bazaar. 'Jackfruit,' he heard her say excitedly to herself. And then, even more excited, so the word came out wrong: 'Cakfurit. But it will give the whole family heart palpitations!'

He could see the old Bengali teacher too, sitting on his string cot by the gate with his typewriter. He typed loudly and when the little bell went off at the end of each line, he paused and read it aloud.

Mr and Mrs Raipur, who lived in the little room at the edge of the big, crumbling Raipur family home, emerged to walk their baby up and down among the canna lilies in their garden.

'Such a beautiful baby,' said Mr Raipur. 'Oh, what a beautiful baby. Look, it has a face just like mine.'

'Not at all like yours,' said Mrs Raipur. And she sang: 'Small nose.' She sang: 'Small nose, pretty rose, tiny mung bean, little little queen.'

Far away, a generator began to roar .

$xy = o$ and $x \neq o$, then $y = o$. If there is x and y and the result is zero. If x is not zero, y is.

Sampath remembered how he had not at any time ever managed to solve a problem put to him by Father Matthew Mathematics, never managed to rake and weed those forests of numbers and letters upon the board into tidy rows following an orderly progression of arrows to a solution that matched the one in the list of answers at the back of the textbook.

Eating jackfruit in the summer causes anxiety and, in some individuals, ill-temper.

'Little star,' sang Mrs Raipur, 'pretty flower. Rose and jasmine and moonflower.'

'And cauliflower,' said Mr Raipur.

'Radishes. Are those radishes? No, potatoes. Potatoes? No, radishes.'

Somewhere a pressure cooker hissed.

Kulfi Chawla climbed the stairs that led from the balcony to the rooftop with a guava. Sorry for her son, she crept up behind him. 'Would you like a guava?' she asked. She had been unable to resist buying it, even though it was the first of the season and still a little hard. She pulled his ear affectionately.

He thought of the post office.

'No,' he wanted to shout. 'No, I do not want any guava,' he wanted to say. But his stomach growled and he took the fruit into his hands. He was cross and grumpy. The guava was cool and green and calm-looking.

The post office. The post office. The post office. It made him want to throw up. He decided not to think of it again.

Guavas are tasty and refreshing and should be eaten whenever possible.

He stared at the fruit, wished he could absorb all its coolness, all its quiet and stillness into him.

'Oh, what should I do?' he asked out loud, all of a sudden. 'What, what, what?' He stared at the guava intently, ferociously, with a fevered gaze, and gave it a shake. He felt it expand in response, rising under his fingertips.

'What should I do?' he said, giving it another desperate shake. 'I do not want a job. I do not like to live like this,' he wailed . . . And suddenly, before his amazed eyes, the surface of the guava rose even more . . . and exploded in a vast Boom! creamy flesh flying, droplets showering high into the sky, seeds scattering and hitting people on the balconies and rooftops, and down on the street.

'Ho!' shouted Lakshmiji, who had been hit in the eye. 'What is going on there? All kinds of bizarre happenings in that household always.'

But she received no answer. Up on the rooftop, Sampath felt his body fill with a cool greenness, his heart swell with a mysterious wild sweetness. He felt an awake clear sap flowing through him, something quite unlike human blood. How do such things happen? He could have sworn a strange force had entered him, that something new was circulating within him. He shuddered in a peculiar manner and then he began to smile.

'Oh dear,' said Kulfi. 'I will complain to the fruit seller, Sampath, beta. Would you like an egg instead?'

Sampath's bare feet were cold against the floor. A breeze lifted the hair off his forehead. Goose bumps covered his arms. He thought of Public Transport, of the Bureau of Statistics, of head massages, of socks and shoes, of interview strategies. Of never ever being left alone, of being unable to sleep and of his father talking and lecturing in the room below.

'No,' Sampath answered. His heart was big inside his chest. 'No, I do not want an egg,' he said. 'I want my freedom.'

6

The afternoon of the next day, the family departed to attend another wedding (for it was the wedding season, you remember), but they left Sampath at home so as to be sure he would not pull down his pants at yet another important event. As soon as they had rounded the corner of the lane on which they lived, Sampath let himself out of the house. Propelled by a great buoyancy of feeling, he made his way down to the bazaar. Here, he caught the first bus he saw.

The bus thundered along on the road leaving Shahkot, the roar of its dirty engine filling the air. Sampath thought of snakes that leave the withered rags of their old skins behind and disappear into grass, their presence unbetrayed by even a buckle in the foliage; of insects that crack pods and clay shells, that struggle from the warm blindness of silk and membrane to be lost in enormous skies. He thought of how he was leaving the world, a world that made its endless revolutions towards nothing. Now it did not matter any more. His heart was caught in a thrall of joy and fear. Somehow, somewhere, he had found a crack. Bus stations and people passed by in a blur.

He had taken the bus that took the milk sellers home after they had brought their milk to be sold in town. Squashed between dozens of cold, empty canisters, he continued all the way to the outskirts of town, until the buildings began to thin and patches of scrub and bedraggled trees appeared. He rode until no buildings could be seen at all, until they climbed up into the undulations of the foothills, so Sampath could feel the air thin about him and the freshness of greenery bloom within his tired frame. They climbed higher and higher.

An old crone moved to sit closer to him. She had so many canisters, he was forced to lean right out of the window and to hang on for dear life. What is more, she was one of those old women who despise a silence. Especially irritated by Sampath's face in its cocoon-like veil, she used her voice like a needle to reach and poke. 'Where do you come from and what is your family name? What does your father do and how much does your uncle earn? How many relatives do you have in your house and how many cupboards? And the way to really good health is to drink a litre of buffalo milk first thing in the morning before the sun rises.'

Sampath felt the marvellous emotion that had overtaken him begin to sag. The bus groaned its way up the slope of the hill. For a brief moment, the engine hiccuped and the bus stopped. In this moment, before the driver changed gears and proceeded up the hillside, Sampath leapt from the window of the stalling bus, spurred by his annoyance at the old crone's voice. Amazed passengers who happened to be looking out at the view as they continued their journey saw Sampath racing into the wilderness towards an old orchard visible far up the slope. He ran with a feeling of great urgency. Over bushes, through weeds. Before him he saw a tree, an ancient tree, silence held between its branches like a prayer. He reached its base and feverishly, without pausing, he began to climb. He clawed his way from branch to branch. Hoisting himself up, he disturbed dead leaves and insect carcasses and all the bits of dried-up debris that collect in a tree. It rained down about him as he clambered

all the way to the top. When he settled among the leaves –
the very moment he did so – the burgeoning of spirits that
had carried him so far away and so high up fell from him
like a gust of wind that comes out of nowhere, rustles
through the trees and melts into nothing like a ghost.

The passengers who happened to be looking out of the
window might have sworn they saw a monkey man leaping in the orchard, causing the leaves to jump and quiver.
But they were tired from selling their milk all morning and
rubbed their eyes before they looked again so as not to be
deceived. By then the bus had left Sampath's tree far
behind and everything was its normal self again.

The tree Sampath had climbed was a guava tree. A guava
tree larger and more magnificent than any he had ever seen
before. It grew in the orchard that had been owned by the
old District Judge of Shahkot, before the government
declared the land to be part of area reserved for national
forest.

Concealed in the branches of the tree he had climbed,
Sampath felt his breathing slow and a wave of peace and
contentment overtook him. All about him the orchard was
spangled with the sunshine of a November afternoon,
webbed by the reflections of the shifting foliage and filled
with a liquid intricacy of sun and shadow. The warmth
nuzzled against his cheek like the muzzle of an animal and,
as his heartbeat grew quiet, he could hear the soft popping
and rustling of plants being warmed to their different
scents all about him. How beautiful it was here, how
exactly as it should be. This orchard matched something he
had imagined all his life: myriad green-skinned globes
growing sweet-sour and marvellous upon a hillside with
enough trees to fill the eye and enough fruit to scent the air.

The leaves of these trees were just a shade darker than the fruit and the bark was a peeling away of tan over a milky paleness so delicate and so smooth that his fingers thrilled to its touch. And these trees were not so big, or so thick with leaves, or so crowded together, as to obscure the sky, which showed clean through the branches. Before his eyes, flitting and darting all about him, was a flock of parrots, a vivid jewel-green, chattering and shrieking in the highest of spirits. This scene filled his whole mind and he wondered if he could ever get enough of it. This was the way of riches and this was a king's life, he thought . . . and he ached to swallow it whole, in one glorious mouthful that could become part of him for ever. Oh, if he could exchange his life for this luxury of stillness, to be able to stay with his face held towards the afternoon like a sunflower and to learn all there was to know in this orchard: each small insect crawling by; the smell of the earth thick beneath the grass; the bristling of leaves; his way easy through the foliage; his tongue around every name. And then, as the afternoons grew quick and smoky and the fruit green-gold and ripe, he'd pick a guava . . . He'd hold it against his cheek and roll it in his palms so as to feel its knobbly surface with a star at its base, its scars that were rough and brown from wind and rain and the sharp beak of some careless bird. And when he finally tasted it, the fruit would not let him down; it would be the most wonderful, the most tasty guava he could ever have eaten . . .

Yes, he was in the right place at last. Tiredness rolled over him like a wave and, closing his eyes, he fell into a deep slumber, lodged in a fork in the guava tree.

7

The day their son moved into a tree, the Chawla family, worried and full of distress, took up residence outside the local police station. They sat on the bench beneath the station's prize yellow rose creeper and waited for news of his whereabouts. That is, the three women sat on the bench while Mr Chawla walked around and around the building, making the policemen dizzy by shouting through every window he passed during his circuits. If he were the Superintendent of Police, he said, Sampath would, right this minute, be back in his usual vegetable-like stupor between them.

The town made the most of the drama. Neighbours came by regularly for news and everyone shouted out their support on their way to and from the market. In some places there are people of quiet disposition and few words, but around Shahkot they were a very rare exception. People visited their friends a great deal, and when they visited their friends, they talked the whole time, and in this way a great deal of information was passed back and forth, from even the most remote and isolated of places.

So although for one awful day it seemed as if Sampath had vanished for ever, the next afternoon the watchman of the university research forest bicycled into town to bring his married sister some curd. Along with the curd, he also brought the news that, in the old orchard outside Shahkot, someone had climbed a tree and had not yet come back down. Nobody could tell why. The man, he said, would answer no questions.

'If someone in this country is crazy enough to climb up a tree, you can be sure it is Sampath,' said Mr Chawla. 'There is no doubting the matter. Thank goodness the property no longer belongs to that judge or he would have Sampath clapped in jail for making a disturbance in his trees. We must just get him down without delay.'

Holding hands, the family ran together to the bus stop, their rubber slippers slapping against their heels. They caught the same bus Sampath had taken on his journey out of Shahkot and got off close to where he had leapt from the window to run up the hillside, and here, far beyond the edge of the town, they made their way down the crisscross of little paths that led into an old orchard that had once borne enough fruit for it to be shipped to and sold in New Delhi. But it had been abandoned for many years now, the fruit acquiring the tang of the wilderness, the branches growing into each other, and these days was used only by an occasional goatherd grazing his flock. The orchard trees stretched almost all the way up the hillside, bordering, at its edge, the university research forest.

With determination and purpose, the Chawla family clacked about, shouting up into the leaves. At last, at the far corner of the farthest guava grove, right near the crumbling wall that bordered the forest, they discovered Sampath sitting in his tree eating a guava, his legs dangling beneath him. He had been watching their efforts with some alarm.

What on earth was he to say? He imagined himself declaring: 'I am happy over here.' Or asking in a surprised fashion: 'But why have you come to visit me?' He could answer their accusations with a defiant: 'But for some people it is normal to sit in trees.' Or, serene with new-found dignity, he could say: 'I am adopting a simple way of life. From now on I have no relatives.' However, he did not wish to hurt anyone's feelings. Perhaps he could leave out the last line and add instead that everybody was his relative. He could hold on to the branches and shout: 'Pull at me all you want, but you'll have to break my arms before I'll let go.' He could scream: 'Try to move a mountain before you try to move me.'

In the end, as it happened, he said nothing at all.

'What are you doing up there?' shouted Mr Chawla. 'Get down at once.'

Sampath looked sturdily into the leafy world about him, trying to steady his wildly fluttering heart. He concentrated on the way the breeze ran over the foliage, like a hand runs over an animal's dark fur to expose a silvery underside.

Pinky felt a sudden surge of embarrassment for her brother. 'Get out of the tree – the whole family is being shamed,' she said bitterly.

'Oh, come down, Sampath, please,' his grandmother exclaimed. 'You are going to fall sick up there. Look at your thin yellow face! We had better take you to the doctor straight away.'

Still, he was silent.

Looking at her son, Kulfi felt the past come rushing back to her, engulfing her in the memory of a time when she was young, when her mind was full of dark corners, when her thoughts grew deep and underground and could not be easily uttered aloud. She remembered the light of a far star in her eyes, an unrecognizable look that had made her a stranger to herself when she stared into the mirror. She remembered the desperation she had sometimes felt, that rose about her as if she were being surrounded and enclosed by an enormous wall. She looked at her son sitting up in the tree and felt her emotions shift, like a vast movement of the spheres, and then she said: 'Let him be.'

'Let him be!' said Mr Chawla. 'Do families allow their sons to climb up trees? You are the number one most strange mother in the world. Your son climbs up a tree and leaves home and you say: "Let him be." With you as his mother, no wonder he has turned out like this. How can I keep normality within this family? I take it as a full-time job and yet it defies possibility. We must formulate a plan. Only monkeys climb up trees.'

Sampath clutched the branch he was sitting on and held it tight.

Monkeys climbed up trees. Beetles lived in trees. Ants crawled up and down them. Birds sat in them. People used them for fruit and firewood, and underneath them they made each other's acquaintance in the few months between the time they got married and the babies arrived. But for someone to travel a long distance just to sit in a tree was preposterous. For that person to be sitting there a few days later was more preposterous still.

In desperation, the family called upon Dr Banerjee from the clinic in the bazaar, and, an energetic man, he arrived as quickly as he could to view his patient. He had a moustache and round glasses and a degree from the medical school in Ranchi. 'Come down,' he shouted good-humouredly. 'How do you expect me to examine you while you're sitting up in a tree?'

But, oh no, Sampath would take no risks. He was not a fool. He would not climb down to be caught and – who knows? – put into a cage and driven off to the insane asylum on Alipur Road, like the madman who had interrupted the ladies' home economics class at the university and been lured and trapped by a single sweet. So, at the family's pleading, Dr Banerjee, who prided himself on being a good sport, hoisted himself into the tree, stethoscope and blood-pressure pump about his neck. He climbed all the way up to Sampath so he could look into his eyes and ears, check his tongue, listen to his heart, take his blood pressure and hit his knee with an expertly aimed karate-like move of his hand. Then he climbed down and got back into the scooter rickshaw he had arrived in. 'He is a crazy person,' he said, beaming, the mirth of the entire situation too much for him. 'Nobody except God can do anything about that.' And he disappeared back into town.

The family went on to see the doctor of Tibetan medicine who had been recommended by their neighbour, Laksh-miji. 'A variety of cures may be prescribed,' he said. 'For example, medicines derived from the scorpion, the sea scorpion, the sea dragon and the sea mouse.'

'What sea mouse?' shouted Mr Chawla. 'There is no such thing as a sea mouse,' and he dragged the family from the dark little clinic, despite their interest in the sea mouse. They went on to the homoeopathic and Ayurvedic doctors, and to the naturopath who lived all the way in Kajuwala.

'Unless he faints from hunger, a diet of millet and sprouts is not going to make Sampath descend from the tree,' said Kulfi firmly, and they decided not to pursue the recommen-dation made by the nature doctor. After all, they did not want to starve Sampath. However, dutifully they pounded pellets into powders, brewed teas and once, twice, some-times ten times a day they counted out the homoeopathic pills that looked and smelled promising but wrought none of the miraculous changes they had been assured of. Finally, they visited the holy man who lived outside the tea stall near the deer park.

'Sorry to disturb you. Our son is afflicted.'

'How is he afflicted?'

'He is suffering from madness.'

'How is he suffering? Is he shouting?'

'No.'

'Having fits?'

'No.'

'Is he tearing his hair out?'

'No.'

'Is he biting his neighbours? Biting himself? Is he sleep-walking? Does he stick out his tongue and roll his eyes? Is he rude to strangers?'

'No. He eats and sleeps and takes good care of his hair. He doesn't shout and he doesn't bite himself. He has never been rude to strangers.'

'Then he does not exhibit any of the sure signs of madness.'

'But he is sitting up in a tree!'

'Arrange a marriage for him. Then you can rest in peace. You will have no further problems.'

It is necessary at some point for every family with a son to acquire a daughter-in-law. This girl who is to marry the son of the house must come from a good family. She must have a pleasant personality. Her character must be decent and not shameless and bold. This girl should keep her eyes lowered and, because she is humble and shy, she should keep her head bowed as well. Nobody wants a girl who stares people right in the face with big froggy eyes. She should be fair-complexioned, but if she is dark the dowry should include at least one of the following items: a television set, a refrigerator, a Godrej steel cupboard and maybe even a scooter. This girl must be a good student and show proficiency in a variety of different fields. When she sings her voice must be honey-sweet and bring tears of joy to the eyes. When she dances people should exclaim 'Wah!' in astounded pleasure. It should be made clear that she will not dance and sing after marriage and shame the family. This girl should have passed all her examinations in the first division but will listen respectfully when her prospective in-laws lecture her on various subjects they themselves failed in secondary school.

She must not be lame. She must walk a few steps, delicately, feet small beneath her sari. She must not stride or kick up her legs like a horse. She must sit quietly, with knees together. She should talk just a little to show she can, but she should not talk too much. She should say just one word, or maybe two after she has been coaxed and begged several times: 'Just a few sentences. Just one sentence.' Her mother should urge: 'Eat something. Eat a laddoo. My daughter made these with her own hands.' And these laddoos must not be recognizable as coming from the sweetmeat shop down the road. The embroidery on the cushion covers the prospective in-laws lean against, and the paintings on the walls opposite, should also be the work of her own hands. They should be colour-coordinated, with designs of fruit and flowers.

She should not be fat. She should be pleasantly plump, with large hips and breasts but a small waist. Though generous and good-tempered, this girl should be frugal and not the sort who would squander the family's wealth. A girl who, though quiet, would be able to shout down the prices of vegetables and haggle with the shopkeepers and spot all their dirty tricks and expose them. Talk of husband and children should so overcome her with shyness and embarrassment that she should hide her face, pink as a rosebud in the fold of her sari.

Then, if she has fulfilled all the requirements for a sound character and impressive accomplishments, if her parents have agreed to meet all the necessary financial contributions, if the fortune tellers have decided the stars are lucky and the planets are compatible, everyone can laugh with relief and tilt her face up by the chin and say she is exactly what they have been looking for, that she will be a daughter to their household. This, after all, is the boy's family. They're entitled to their sense of pride.

But the family could find only one prospective daughter-in-law. She was scrawny and dark. 'Like a crow,' said Kulfi and Ammaji indignantly when the first photograph was shown to them by Lakshmiji, who was acting as marriage broker. 'You are trying to marry poor Sampath to a crow.'

'He is lucky to find anyone at all,' said Mr Chawla, who had given up all hope of motor scooters and wedding parties at the Hans Raj Hotel.

The girl arrived along with her family on the public bus. Apart from her family, the bus was full of singing ladies and gentlemen, pilgrims returning from a trip to the Krishna temple in a neighbouring town. The Chawlas watched as the bus veered off the road like a crazy beetle and moved towards them in a cloud of dust.

The bus driver had obligingly offered to drop off the family right at Sampath's orchard. A bride-to-be should not have to walk and grow dusty and be shown to disadvantage, he said sympathetically. He himself had a daughter to marry. And: 'Yes, yes, let's take them directly to the boy,' chorused the other passengers, pausing to make this decision before resuming their singing. They clapped their hands to keep the song moving along; their hair flew; they swayed from side to side, partly for the sake of rhythm, partly because of the way the bus leapt and shook through potholes and bumps. They closed their eyes and let their voices rise and flutter from the bus to the Chawlas waiting under Sampath's tree. 'Ten ways to cook rice,' they sang, 'seventeen flowering trees in the forest, twenty hermits at my table. But those who know say you take forms beyond number. O Lord, teach me the way of infinite marvel.'

The air rushed up through the cracks in the bus, up their saris and trousers, so that a pleasant breeze circulated around their legs. Everybody looked very puffed up, wobbling as if some large force inside them were trying to break free.

Despite the driver's kindness and the attention she had received with the help of a handkerchief, a little spit and a large amount of talcum powder, the girl descended from the bus looking extremely dusty. The pilgrims, curious about what might happen during this unusual encounter between prospective marriage partners, tumbled out of the bus as well, in a messy and chaotic heap. They needed a break for lunch anyway, and a little private time behind some foliage. Holding the prospective bride before them like a gift, the group moved towards the guava tree. Sampath had always had a soft spot for the lady on the label of the coconut hair-oil bottle. He had spent rather a large amount of time in consideration of her mysterious smile upon the bathroom shelf. While squatting upon the mildewed wooden platform taking his bucket baths, he had conducted a series of imagined encounters with her, complete with imagined conversations and imagined quarrels and reconciliations. She would meet him wreathed in the scent of the oil, with a smile as white as the gleaming inside of a coconut. A braid of hair had travelled downwards from the top of the coconut lady's head and followed the undulations of the bottle. Sampath looked down at the veiled woman standing underneath his tree and felt hot and horrified.

'Please come down and be introduced. You have sat in the tree long enough,' said Mr Chawla.

Sampath thought he might faint.

'Climb up, daughter,' the girl's father urged her. 'Climb up. Come on, one step. Just a step.'

The devotees raised the girl's rigid, unwilling form into the tree. 'Up,' they urged, and slowly she began to climb. She was encased in layers of shiny material, like a large, expensive toffee. The cloth billowed about her, making her look absurdly stout. Her gold slippers slipped with every step. Her sari was pulled over her head and she held the edge of it between her teeth so as to keep as much of her face modestly covered as possible. It seemed an eternity before she neared Sampath. It was clear that this girl would not take well to life in a tree. She paused and looked back down for further directions. Nobody knew quite what to expect, or how she should proceed. Even Mr Chawla was at a loss as to what should happen next.

'Touch his feet,' someone finally shouted in a moment of inspiration.

'Yes, touch his feet,' the rest of the pilgrims cried, and, extending a single timid finger, like a snail peeping from its shell, she gingerly poked at Sampath's toe. Her finger was as cold as ice and moist. Sampath leapt up in horror. In an equal state of distress, the girl let out a faint cry. Losing her balance and her gold slippers, she tumbled indecorously towards the ground, accompanied by the more robust cries of the pilgrims and her family, who rushed at her with arms outstretched. But they failed to catch her as she fell and she landed with a dull thump upon the ground.

– 61 –

The signs for marriage were not auspicious.

The devotees propped her up against a tree and fanned her with a leafy branch.

'What am I to do with this boy?' Mr Chawla threw his hands up in the air. 'Tell me what I should do? The best education. A job. A wife. The world served to him on a platter, but, oh no, none of it is good enough for him. Mister here must run and sit in a tree. He is not in the least bit thankful for all that has been done for him.'

The girl began to sneeze in tiny mouse-like squeals.

'Stop fanning her with that dirty branch,' someone shouted. 'All the dust must have gone up her nose.'

'Dust or no dust, it is yet one more inauspicious sign,' said another onlooker.

Pinky felt terribly scornful of this third-rate woman who had responded to this important moment by sneezing and whimpering. She gave her a good pinch from behind, hoping to see her jump, but the girl continued to squeak and sniffle. Ammaji ran up with a tin can full of water and emptied it over her just in case the sun had become too strong for her to take. The talcum powder ran in a milky river down her face.

'What can I do?' Mr Chawla repeated. 'What am I to do with this boy?' He was sweating despite the pleasant breeze that wafted about them, laden with the scent of earth and burgeoning vegetation.

He himself had been his son's age when he was married. Kulfi had been even younger, so alarming her family with her weird ways, they were worried that if her marriage were delayed any longer, she would be left on their hands for ever, her sanity dissipating, the sense scattering from her like seeds from a poppy pod. They had spent night after sleepless night gathered at the window to watch as she wandered up and down in the garden, having taken suddenly, after her twentieth birthday, to sleepwalking.

Her father watched pale in his pyjamas; the aunties shook in their petticoats. The months had gone by with no sign of this behaviour abating. The moon grew big, then delicate – a hair's strand, then once more to fullness. Kulfi walked serenely by the bottle-brush trees, barefoot, with the gait of a queen; asleep, but eating slices of melon, spitting out seeds that showered like raindrops among the bushes. In the mornings they discovered apple cores and walnut shells under her bed, sticky trails leading from the kitchen pots straight into her room. In her pockets they found bits of cinnamon and asafoetida. In her hair, little twigs and often a crushed night beetle. But she woke refreshed, with no recollection of her nightly rambles, her midnight feasting, insisting she had slept soundly when her family, grey and dizzy from lack of sleep, questioned her over the morning tea. In the garden watermelons grew in a tangle they hacked at in vain.

Clearly she was going mad. Yes, there it was – the eccentricity that had plagued her mother's side of the family for generations bubbling up yet again, just when they hoped the culprit genes had finally run into some dead end and been laid to rest. Again and again it had surprised them, appearing haphazardly in the most stable of uncles, the newest of babies. There had been a grandfather who loved his chickens so passionately he insisted on sleeping in the coop at night; an aunt who announced she was the last Maharaja of Oudh just when it had been decided that the family seemed sane at last; a child that spoke only its own garbled language . . .

When it became apparent that Kulfi too had inherited

this familial strain of lunacy, her father knew he had not a moment to lose. And before the news of her oddity was carried to the bazaar by the washerman or the bottle and jar man or any visitors who might happen to see or overhear anything suspicious, he learned that widowed Ammaji in the far-off town of Shahkot was looking for a match for her son; and even though they were from a family of a much lower class, he offered them a dowry they could not refuse.

But even so!

'That crazy family!' Mr Chawla had exclaimed. 'Oh no. Absolutely not. I am not going to get married to their daughter. I am staying well away from that sort of thing, thank you very much.'

But Ammaji clucked her tongue. For some reason she had taken a liking to the girl, and who on earth would turn down a big sum of money like the one they had been offered? It would allow them to clear all their generation's debts and buy a refrigerator. 'Don't be so unreasonable,' she said. 'She appears normal, even if she is a little bit shy.'

'With these things, there is no knowing,' said Mr Chawla. 'In fact, it is the quiet ones you have to watch out for.'

But although he did not admit it out loud, he too had been smitten by Kulfi's flower beauty, her slender frame, her impossible delicacy so different from the robustness of the neighbourhood girls with their loud laughter, their round hips, their sly nudging and winking. And in a few months' time Kulfi moved from her ancestral home, which was big and rambling, even if the roofs leaked and the paint had peeled away, to the Chawlas' tiny rooms in the tumbledown streets of Shahkot. And over time Mr Chawla had developed a sort of exasperated affection for his wife, even when it became apparent that she was not the normal daughter of a crazy family as Ammaji had conjectured, but the crazy daughter of a crazy family as he himself had surmised. He was almost always right. With a wife like this, and two children to look after and manage, Mr Chawla grew more and more firmly established in his role as head of the family, and as this fitted his own idea of the way he ought to live, it gave him secret satisfaction despite all his complaining.

He was the head of a family and he liked it that way.

But oh! What good was it to be the head of a family when you had a son who ran and sat in a tree? Who slipped from beneath your fingers and shamed you?

'What am I do?' he demanded of the devotees still milling about, to show them it was not for lack of effort and concern on his behalf that Sampath had ended up in such a pitiful state. He hit his forehead with the flat of his palm, for drama has a way of overriding the embarrassment of a situation that should be privately experienced.

The ladies and gentlemen from the bus felt a little sorry for him. 'Yes, yes, how shameful,' they muttered. 'And coming from a decent family and all. Clearly the boy has been derailed.'

They focused on Sampath, watching to see how his father's distress would affect him. Surely any son, even this one, would respond to such a moving show of emotion.

Sensitive to the atmosphere of expectation beneath him, Sampath looked into the upturned eyes of the devotees. He thought of his old school and the post office and entire roomfuls of people awaiting the answer to questions he had often not even heard. He wondered how it could be that he had never felt comfortable among people. Here he was alone, caught up in the enigmatic rituals of another species. 'Go on with your own lives,' he wanted to shout. 'Go on, go on. Leave me to mine.'

But, of course, he could not say any such thing. In desperation he looked around him. Among the crowd of faces down below, he recognized that of Mr Singh, the brother-in-law of a neighbour in Shahkot. Mr Singh, whose letters he had sometimes read in idle moments in the post office. As if in a frantic plea for help, he shouted: 'Mr Singhji.'

He remembered one particular letter sent by him to his father.

'Is your jewellery still safely buried beneath the tulsi plant?'

Mr Singh turned pale. 'How do you know about my circumstances?' he asked.

Sampath then caught sight of Mrs Chopra. 'How is that lump in your throat that travels up and down your windpipe, whispering threats and almost bursting right out of your chest?'

'Hai,' she gasped. 'Who told you?'

Encouraged now by his success, Sampath's face was brightening a little. He jabbed his finger at a bald-headed man in the crowd and said: 'And you, sir, that secret oil you got from the doctor in Side Gully. Clearly it is not working. Try a good massage with mustard oil and your hair will sprout as thick and as plentiful as grass in the Cherrapunjee rain.'

Their eyes wide with what they had seen, important in the news they were carrying, the devotees drove back into Shahkot.

There was a man up in the guava tree, a remarkable man. He had known all sorts of things. The dacoits were blackmailing poor Mr Singh. An evil spirit had established itself in Mrs Chopra's stomach. Ratan Sinha had been using a special hair oil to no effect.

Clearly, there was more to this post-office clerk than to ordinary mortals. In his eyes they had detected a rare spirit.

'Post-office clerk climbs tree,' Mr Chawla read to his astounded family a little later in the week when the story had reached even the local news bureau and been deemed worthy of attention. 'Fleeing duties at the Shahkot post office, a clerk has been reported to have settled in a large guava tree. According to popular speculation, he is one of an unusual spiritual nature, his child-like ways being coupled with unfathomable wisdom.'

There it was – a modest column introducing Sampath to the world, along with news of a scarcity of groundnuts, an epidemic of tree frogs and the rumour that Coca-Cola might soon be arriving in India.

8

It was at this point in time that Mr Chawla had a realization – all of a sudden, with a tumble and rush of understanding – a realization so quick and so incredible in nature that his heart was caught in a constant state of pounding. Sampath might make his family's fortune. They could be rich! How many hermits were secretly wealthy? How many holy men were not at all the beggars they appeared to be? How many men of unfathomable wisdom possessed unfathomable bank accounts? What an opportunity had arisen out of nowhere! Already there was a change in the way people looked at Sampath: no longer did they snigger and smirk or make sympathetic noises with their tongues. He, Mr Chawla, must move as quickly as he could to claim these possibilities for his family, possibilities that stretched, he was sure, well beyond his sight's furthest horizon. He dropped his plans to return to Shahkot as soon as possible, Sampath in tow, and began to think of the old watchman's shed the family was camping in as a permanent residence. He kept his thoughts close to his chest, however, and didn't say a word to anyone, but in a sudden turnabout of policy that both surprised and pleased his wife and mother, who were already settling into the orchard as if it were their own long-lost home, he stopped berating Sampath for having climbed up the tree, and turned his attention to other matters.

In his attempt to make Sampath more comfortable so that he might greet visitors in a style that matched his father's vision of the future, Mr Chawla recruited the help of Pinky, Ammaji and Kulfi. They considered the problem with due seriousness and spent many hours discussing the practicalities of the matter while sipping endless glasses of milky tea. Would it be nice for him to have a hammock? A length of cloth strung between branches? No, that would not be grand enough. Besides, Sampath would be forever horizontal and, after all, he was young and healthy, so surely he should not be allowed such indulgences. How about a platform? 'Perhaps later,' said Mr Chawla, 'when we can afford some wood and get a carpenter. Constructing a platform is beyond us.' They could not construct a tree house either. Anyway: 'Nothing doing,' interjected Sampath at this point in their conversation. 'I am not going to live in a house after all this effort to run away from houses.' In the end they decided that for now they would settle for a string cot in the branches upon which Sampath might recline. They raised the cot up to where Sampath sat, Ammaji and Kulfi handing it up to Mr Chawla and Pinky, who climbed all about Sampath.

Less fussy than they were in attempting to ascertain the best position for his new bed and eager for them to leave his domain, Sampath waited impatiently until the cot was wedged into place and anchored with rope; then he settled on to it with great relief, for he had found it uncomfortable to sleep upon a hard trunk. It had left his bones tender, his skin bruised, his muscles pulled in all the wrong directions, arms and legs and various parts of his body falling asleep and then filling him with a painful thrumming when he happened to move again. He adjusted himself constantly and once, to his shame, descended from the tree to sleep upon the grass, scuttling back up just before his family emerged from where they were cosily buried under quilts in the watchman's shed.

One day, on a trip to the bazaar, Mr Chawla spotted a large striped garden umbrella that had been discarded by the Club for Previous Members of the Court. It had been picked up by the umbrella repair man, who was about to use it for parts, when Mr Chawla persuaded him to clean it, patch it and repair the spokes. After it had been spruced up a little, it too was raised into the guava tree. Although it was a bit shabby, it was big enough to shield Sampath and his entire cot from sun and rain. And though it was faded, its yellow and green stripes and scalloped trim still possessed a jaunty air.

Thus Sampath was gradually provided with all sorts of comforts and, the more elaborate his living arrangements, the happier he was. He made a lovely picture, seated there amidst the greenery, reclining upon his cot at a slight angle to the world; propped against numerous cushions; tucked up, during chilly evenings, in a glamorous satin quilt covered with leopard-skin spots, chosen by Ammaji in the bazaar. On his head, he sported a tea-cosy-like red woollen hat, also given to him by Ammaji, who had knitted it and raised it to him on a stick. He was particularly fond of this hat, for it kept his head snug and warm at night when the breeze was chilly, and it kept the night rustlings, the crawling of little black beetles, ants and moths, out of his ears as well.

'I'm comfortable,' he announced to his family with a wave of his hand, as if dismissing them now that he found everything to his satisfaction. This left them bewildered for a minute, since they were yet to get used to this reversal in their relationship. How they had scolded him once upon a time for every little thing he had done. Now here he was waving at them as if he were a raja wishing to be left alone. When they were needed again, he summoned them with shouts, starting at dawn, when he desired his morning tea, and then a little later, when he was ready for his bath, which required elaborate arrangements to be made by the whole family, who were, after all, willing to do quite a bit of work in this regard, for they had always been a clean family. Yes, whatever other faults they might have had, nobody could have called them dirty, and they were determined that nobody should have cause to do so now, even if Sampath was in the guava tree.

It took an hour or more before preparations for his bath were finished. Clothed in his striped pair of undershorts, Sampath would sit on his string cot, the quilts and cushions hanging on far branches to air, while Ammaji heated up an enormous pot of water over the fire. Bucketfuls were then raised to Sampath via a rope levering system designed especially for this purpose by his father. Up and down the family ran, with Mr Chawla shouting orders that nobody paid attention to. 'Don't let the fire go out. Rub yourself with oil before you soap yourself. Soap well, Sampath.' The bucket would tilt at the pull of a string from down below, and the water would pour down, a steaming shower that caught the early-morning light and came down like molten lava. Then, enjoying his leisure, Sampath would sit wrapped in a blanket and dry his hair in the strengthening sun while his breakfast was being seen to.

When it came to his meals, all Pinky's efforts in climbing up with bowls and dishes had ended more often in accidents than success, with his dinner either in the grass or, worse, splattered and scalding, over the poor bearer of food. 'Oh no,' Sampath would say sadly as his growling stomach echoed his distress. It took several tries before he was able to eat anything at all. Anxiously, the family would watch as Pinky hoisted herself from branch to branch, holding aloft a pot of dal, a bit of naan between her teeth. 'Careful, beti, careful,' but – splash! – by the time Pinky reached Sampath, there wouldn't be more than a puddle at the bottom of the pot and the naan would be hard and cold with a few bites taken out of it, for, after all, Pinky had needed a little something to keep her going.

'This is absurd,' said Mr Chawla. 'This isn't working.' And made the journey himself one time. 'Stupid naan,' he cursed when it fell from his lips. 'Stupid dal,' he said as a bit sloshed over his fingers, but when the dal pot overturned altogether and landed, boiling hot, upon his tender foot, he erupted in anger. The next day he attached an old wooden crate to the same elementary pulley system used to deliver Sampath's bath water and thereafter Sampath's meals were given to him simply by pulling on a rope and raising the crate. As the fluffy chapattis and naans were made down below, they were proffered to him speared atop a bamboo stick, as were slices of pickle, bits of fruit and other tasty titbits.

Every now and then another crate was attached to the pulley system containing earthenware pots with the help of which Sampath answered the call of nature in as convenient and hygienic a way possible without having to visit the outhouse Mr Chawla had constructed. This worked well, for the pots were disposable, of course, and Sampath was able to pull his umbrella down as a shield so he might sit on them in peace. For a nominal fee, the potter began to deliver batches of new ones at regular intervals.

Thus ensconced in his orchard bower, still not quite able to believe the serendipitous way things had turned out, Sampath gave what came to be known as The Sermon in the Guava Tree, where he responded to people's queries with such charm and wit they were to be his trademark for ever after. They were a mysterious charm and wit, of course, but they were apparent to all those who arrived in growing numbers to see him, making their way down the narrow path to stare with amazement at this skinny, long-legged apparition amidst the leaves.

Among the first to make this trip were Miss Jyotsna and Mr Gupta.

'He must have gone through a thorough and complete transformation,' said Miss Jyotsna. 'Look how his face is so different now.'

Certainly it was a happier, calmer face. 'Namasteji,' said Sampath, greeting them cheerfully from his cot in the trees, his new position of power. Really, he thought, he was quite fond of them. They had always meant well, unlike many others he could name.

'Hello, Sampath,' said Mr Gupta. 'Why did you not take me with you? I could have had a little rest from this one here.' He pointed at Miss Jyotsna with a comic expression upon his face.

'Any time you want a rest from her you should send her to the sari and salwar kameez shop,' laughed Sampath. 'You know how much this lady loves clothes . . . Oh, but maybe that is not such a good idea. Already she owes the Ladies' Fashion Shop 152 rupees and eighty paisa.'

Once when Miss Jyotsna had been summoned to Mr D. P. S.'s office, Sampath had had the chance to examine the contents of her purse: the lipstick and comb, the embroidered handkerchief, the receipts and safety pins, the toffees and small vials of homoeopathic medicine . . .

Miss Jyotsna raised a trembling hand to her mouth. The blood rushed to her face. She had kept her debt to the sari shop a strict secret. What else could Sampath say about her? She had heard of the way he had stunned the devotees of the Krishna temple with his clairvoyance; now he had used his powers to examine her.

She nudged Mr Gupta with her elbow. 'Treat him with some respect,' she said, surprising him with the new note of reverence in her voice. She was apparently awe-struck by what she saw. And even the paan-shop man, who had also come to visit, thinking that maybe he would sell a few paans while satisfying his curiosity, turned to give Mr Gupta a dirty look and said, 'It seems you are unversed in spiritual matters.'

'But it is only Sampath,' protested Mr Gupta.

But clearly it was not only Sampath. It was Sampath of unfathomable wisdom, sitting in his tree abode.

The sweet-shop man joined them after work, then two college students skipping a lecture, the washerman on his bicycle and a pregnant lady who wished to know if her baby would be a boy or a girl. 'Ah yes,' she said with satisfaction to those standing about the tree with her, 'he has the same expression as the Tajewala sage in samadhi. Perhaps you have seen the photographs?'

'My son is keeping bad company,' interrupted a distressed but spirited relative of Lakshmiji's dressed in a canary-yellow sari. 'What can I do?'

'Add lemons to milk and it will grow sour,' answered Sampath in an exceptionally sociable and happy temper, mimicking the old men of Shahkot, who liked to sit at their gates on winter afternoons, basking in their socks and hats, while they lectured passers-by. 'But add some sugar, madam, and Wah! how good that milk will taste. These are things I do not have to tell you. You yourself know you behaved just like your son when you were young.'

He impressed himself by how many details he had stowed away while reading in the post office. Why, he could just pull them out of some secret compartment in his brain the way a magician pulls rabbits from a hat. How admiringly the people below the tree were looking at him! Never before had he felt the sweet and unique pleasure of giving advice that now suffused his being and shone about his face.

'By this do you mean I should remove him from the presence of these undesirable characters?' Lakshmiji's relative asked.

'If you put a chicken on the fire and leave it, in a little while it will no longer be a chicken, but ash and bones. Leave a kettle on the flames, the water will grow hot and then, if someone does not lift it off, it will all boil away until there is nothing left. If your child is playing with a dead smelly mouse, you will not debate: "Should I let him be, should I let him play?" No, you will throw away the mouse and take your child indoors to wash his hands.'

Mr Chawla and Pinky, who had just arrived from a trip to the market in time to hear this last sentence, looked at each other in disbelief when they saw how closely people listened to Sampath.

'Did you hear?' Mr Chawla asked Pinky.

'Dead smelly mouse?' said Pinky, incredulous.

'If you do not weed,' said Sampath, 'your tomato plant will not flower.'

Ammaji and Kulfi, flushed with pride, were already part of the crowd. They listened to every word that was being uttered, leaning forward to hear a round-faced man ask: 'I am being overtaken by spiritual matters. How can I keep my mind on my responsibilities?'

'If you talk to a young girl as she stands before the mirror, it is like talking to a deaf person. And can you keep a moth from flying into the lantern by saying she should worry about her three children?'

'But are you saying I should forgo my duties to my wife and children?'

'Once my uncle had a rooster and an insect laid its eggs in the flesh of its rear end. It knew the young ones would have a warm place to live and plenty to eat before they were old enough to leave.'

'Which is the better way to realize God? The way of devotion or the way of knowledge?'

The questions came fast and furious.

'Some people can only digest fish cooked in a light curry. Others are of a sour disposition and should not eat pickled fish. In the south they enjoy fish cooked with coconut water. I myself have a preference for pomfret in a sauce of chilli and tamarind thickened with gram flour.'

'Where can I begin my search? What is the starting point?'

Sampath smiled; then he yawned and pulled his hat over his eyes. He was growing tired and so, as quickly and easily as a child, he went to sleep.

A hushed silence overcame the visitors. Kulfi got up soundlessly and slipped away to begin cooking Sampath's dinner. In Shahkot she had cooked only now and then when inspiration mounted somewhere out in the sea of her unconscious and rushed up to swallow her like a tidal wave.

But how could she possibly have reconciled her wild dreams with her tame life in Shahkot, with their tiny kitchen, their meals on the old plastic-covered table? Again and again, the dishes she produced could not match the

-76-

visions inside her; she could not be satisfied with the ingredients that came bottled and packaged on store shelves or withered in bazaar baskets; the kitchen was too small for the scale of operation she desired; her cooking was constantly interrupted by neighbours investigating the smells that wafted into their houses from her stove. 'Don't mix fish with chicken,' they advised her. 'Fry the onions first and then add the garlic later. Keep the milk aside until the very end of cooking.' The frustration inside her would grow into an enormous cloud that blocked off everything else and her eyesight and hearing would go blurry. Sampath would taste what she made, and smile and nod his admiration, but she would be inconsolable. It was all wrong, all wrong. It took her weeks to calm down, sitting with Sampath on the rooftop in complete silence. Months later, when the tidal wave of inspiration came again, the entire event would repeated.

Mr Chawla had learned to shrug his shoulders at her. All his early attempts to teach her to interact normally with the world had made as much impression on her as rain on waterproofing and instead, as soon as Sampath was old enough, he had turned his attention to his son, for his greatest responsibility, he felt, was to pummel him into being at least minimally functional in the world. There had been one or two occasions, of course, when he had been made very worried, like the time when Kulfi tried to steal the experimental plants from the agricultural centre's annual display, or when she had attempted to get into the cage of rare pheasants in the tiny Shahkot zoo so she could catch and cook one. Each time she had been caught by guards, who assumed she was just a straying visitor and one only as bothersome as all the rest of the boisterous crowd. And luckily these events had not often been repeated.

Ammaji too left Kulfi to herself, apart from a few muttered comments and laments that were her duty as a mother-in-law. She was secretly pleased by how her place in the household and in Mr Chawla's life had not been altered at all when Kulfi had arrived. Some poor women suffered the fate of having their sons turn their backs on them and ignore them completely after marriage.

Here, in the orchard, the hold of other people on Kulfi and her awareness of them retreated even further and, like Sampath, she discovered the relief of space. Inspired by the forest, she had embarked upon a series of experiments, a fervent crusade to bring her fantastic imaginings into being. She cooked outdoors, in the sunshine, under the gigantic sky. She felt she was on the brink of something enormous. All around her was a landscape she understood profoundly, that she could comprehend without thought or analysis. She understood it like she understood her son, without conversation or the need to construct a connection or to maintain it. Pinky was a stranger to her, made her nervous and even scared sometimes; it was lucky she was so independent. But Sampath she *knew*. She knew why he was sitting in a tree. It was the right place for him to be; that is where he belonged.

Whenever she saw him upon his cot, saw his face peeking from between the leaves, she was reminded of the day when he was born, his birth mingling in her memory with the wildest storm she had ever witnessed, with the arrival of famine relief and the silver miracle of rain. There, in the midst of the chaos, her son's face had contained an exquisite peace, an absorption in a world other than the one he had been born into.

She cooked only for Sampath, leaving Ammaji to cater to the rest of the family, for his was the only judgement Kulfi trusted.

Almost all day she worked, trying this and that, producing, even in these early days of apprenticeship to her imagination, meals of such flavour and rarity that others could merely guess at what they were missing by the smells that rose from her pots, so intoxicating them by evening's end that they had barely any recollection of what had passed when they departed from their audience with Sampath. They felt filled, though, with a sense of magic and well-being. By the look of Sampath, he too was permeated with a similar feeling, but to a much greater degree. His cheeks grew slowly plumper day by day; his tense, worried expression melted into one of contentment; the soft movement of the days and nights rising and falling about him were gently reflected in his face and his eyes mirrored the quiet of the distant hills.

9

'What about my typing course?' Pinky asked her father one morning not long after The Sermon in the Guava Tree, when it had become apparent, she thought, that no one cared that the life of Pinky Chawla in Shahkot had been rudely interrupted by Sampath's move up the hillside. A week or two was all very well, but she had come to the conclusion that it did not appeal to her as a permanent arrangement.

But Mr Chawla had his mind on other matters. He had been given extended compassionate leave from work, and that meant he would have enough time to see if his secret plans for Sampath – and indeed, for their entire family – could work. Absent-mindedly, he said to his daughter: 'Of what use is that? Really, it is silly to take a class for a such a simple matter.'

This was most unfair of him, for he himself had been the one to lecture her not so very long ago: 'It is very important for young girls to know something useful, not just sit at home and get married. This is the modern India. You should take a typing course.'

Pinky was not interested in typing, and she certainly did not wish to do anything useful in modern India, but she was well aware of the necessity of putting in an appearance in the bazaar every day. If you did not do so, your place in the hierarchy of things, indeed your very identity in the social sphere, would be totally obliterated. Now, condemned to a once-a-week trip undertaken to collect supplies, visit the bank, the post office and other such places for which it was necessary to go into town, she realized she would have to make the most of her meagre opportunities, and these trips became the high point of her existence in the orchard.

'Shall I wear this?' she would mutter to herself beforehand. 'No, no, I'll wear that. No, the colour is wrong. It is too dark for a young girl. Oh, the colour is wrong.' The entire week before each day in town was spent deciding what to wear and she started on the apparel for the next trip as soon as she got home from the bus stop, fussing with needle and thread, washing soap and starch. She knew she was at a disadvantage with a mother who was incapable of going shopping for clothes, who could not discuss which ensemble should be worn to which event and what trinket matched what pair of slippers. Ammaji's tastes were a century behind the times and her father and Sampath were of no help either. She was all alone in this attempt to maintain her position in bazaar society. The outfits of choice were washed and hung to dry over lantana bushes, then placed beneath the tin trunks overnight to smooth out as many wrinkles as possible. When she appeared in the glory of her efforts, she looked as if she were about to enter a fashion show. Her dupattas fluttered behind her in diaphanous waves against the landscape and large quantities of costume jewellery shone and glinted about her face, which was powdered pink and white. Really, it was quite inappropriate for a trip to the market. Furthermore, she had developed the peculiar habit of insisting she was being followed. Someone need only brush past her or glance at her as she walked in the street and Pinky would announce when she got back: 'All the way home a man followed me, staring with big goggly eyes.'

Mr Chawla worried that she was growing a bit soft in the head, living so far out of Shahkot. No doubt if someone put such an effort into matters of clothing and appearance, she would expect a dramatic response, which she might have to invent if it did not happen of its own accord. This was a very dangerous thing and should be nipped in the bud immediately, he felt. 'First you dress up as if you are going to enter the Miss India,' he told her, 'and then you complain that people are staring at you. Of course people will stare if you make such a spectacle of yourself. But as for following you, it is all in your head. Dressing up like that and feeling so self-conscious! If somebody happens to cough, you are sure he has spent all morning following you.' He insisted Pinky make all future trips to the bazaar dressed in simple cotton devoid of gold trims and gaudy flowers, with a face as scrubbed and clean – which meant, of course, as plain and ugly – as it could be.

'You are over-reacting,' said Pinky. How on earth could she be seen in public looking so drab? How dare he curb her taste in fashion? It was enough to throw her into hysterics, but she controlled herself. 'Maybe,' she said, retrenching in a last effort to be allowed her dignity, 'maybe, after all, nobody has been following me.'

But, deciding she needed to be taught moderation and good sense, her father reiterated his insistence that she dress soberly. In initiation of this new look, she should, he pronounced, accompany her grandmother to buy a new pair of dentures in town, for recently Ammaji had decided her life was incomplete without them.

'Look at that old Shantiji,' she would say. 'She has no difficulty eating. Her family takes good care of her. Every year they buy her a new pair of dentures. As I said, they take good care of her. Did you see the way she cracked that bone and gobbled down the marrow? Of course, I didn't have any . . . Well, lucky for her that her family takes such good care of her.'

If she hinted in this fashion, thought Ammaji, no doubt she would finally get what she wanted. A hint should be indirect, it was true, but it should also be clear or it would go unnoticed and be a useless sort of hint.

'If you want dentures, then you can have dentures,' said Mr Chawla in order to keep his mother quiet. Would his family ever leave him alone so he might plot and plan their future in peace? If it were up to them, the new possibilities of Sampath's fame would remain forever untapped and unexploited. However, of course it was true that he wished all improvements for his family. 'There is no need for old people to suffer any more,' he said grandly, as if this substitute for teeth had been his idea in the first place.

Feeling so dowdy she could have cried, Pinky stomped after her grandmother to the bus stop. Unlike her granddaughter, Ammaji was in fine temper. The air outside the town was cool and clean, and reminded her of her childhood. Her grandson was proving to be a great success, just as she had always thought he would be. And she was going to get some dentures.

'After we get the dentures,' she said generously to Pinky, 'we can go and see *Love Story '85.'* Surely a good movie would improve Pinky's spirits. It had been hard to sit in the bus with someone so sour and unwilling to talk. Really, she reflected, Pinky was too headstrong. If she did not get her own way, she sulked and tried to make everybody else feel bad as well. And the trouble with those who did this was that, in the end, unable to stand their sulking, people gave way to them and they got all sorts of presents and treats. It was the good-natured people who suffered in this world. Nobody paid any attention to them. For example, look at the way she had been ignored about the dentures. Months and months, no, indeed years, had gone by in discomfort and deprivation. However, of course, she was not one to sulk and complain.

Praying she would not be seen by any of her acquaintances or the other girls from the polytechnic, Pinky dragged Ammaji through a dark maze of filthy side streets, insisting on taking the back road into the main bazaar area so she would be seen by as few people as possible, her nerves taut, her eyes on the look-out for potential incidents where she might be shamed before some fancy fashion plate of an acquaintance who didn't deserve the pleasure of witnessing Pinky's humiliation.

The denture lady had a whole array of dentures spread out before her on a mat in the corner of the bazaar, between the fish lady and the woman with the plastic buckets. Undeterred by the smell of fish, Ammaji squatted down on the mat and tried them all on. One too big, others too small . . . Finally there was one that seemed somewhat to fit.

'Yes, yes,' said the denture woman, 'it will be fine. It is better that they are a little loose than a little tight.'

Ammaji donned the new gadget, moving and distorting her lips over the unfamiliar expanse of plastic, smacking her two new rows of teeth against each other appreciatively.

It was only later that they ran into a bit of misfortune.

They had emerged from the cinema with Pinky feeling somewhat mollified by the thrilling scenes she had just witnessed between hero and heroine amidst mounting obstacles of dread and terror. This *Love Story* was a film beyond compare! When it first came out, the line of people waiting to get in had snaked all the way from the ticket booth to the university gates, travelling around corners and, blocking traffic, stretching across streets. The crowds nicknamed the heroine Thunder Thighs and went again and again to see her cavort in the famous waterfall scene. There, in defiance of parental wishes and differences in income, religion and caste specifications, she sang in the spray with her beloved, matching him only in the supreme attributes of true love and good looks. There was nothing better than to watch a satisfying drama, one that caused your blood to run strong and red again. Ammaji and Pinky emerged strengthened into the late afternoon and stopped at the Hungry Hop Kwality Ice Cream van for ice cream.

It was at this moment that Pinky spotted the Cinema Monkey! The Cinema Monkey who had so long been harassing the ladies of the town for peanut cones. There it was, loping its way towards them! Hai Rama, how on earth could they have possibly forgotten? Coming to the movie without strong and able chaperons! This would have to happen to them. The monkey came closer. He was so bold, he showed not the slightest trepidation. Any human thief would be feeling a little awkward, robbing like this in broad daylight. The monkey's brown eyes were cold and cruel, red-rimmed and fixed firmly upon them. In a rush of terror, her heart falling into a black nothingness, Pinky shouted: 'Run, run, run. Run, Ammaji. Drop the ice cream and run!'

But Ammaji, who had just been handed a nice chocolate cone by the Hungry Hop boy, ran with the cone – not that this mattered, for the monkey ignored her and ran after

Pinky instead, even though she was without any food products whatsoever. He grabbed hold of her dupatta and held tight as she screamed like a train and pounded down the bazaar street, followed by the gallant Hungry Hop boy, who had been aroused from his usual placid state by their cries of alarm. After all, it was not as if he did not know how to behave in such situations. He too was a regular at the cinema.

Now, inexplicably, for reasons best known to herself, Ammaji decided in the midst of all this confusion, this raised dust and running, to take a bite of her ice-cream cone. As she did so, the dentures, which had been unsettled by so much activity, were dislodged from her gums. Stuck in the ice cream, they leered at her horribly like a ghastly cartoon: skeleton teeth mocking, beckoning from the chocolate mound, an affront to her old age.

Horrified, Ammaji dropped the cone and, mistaking it for his favourite peanuts in a roll of paper, the monkey turned his attention towards her, caught hold of the denture-laden cone and rushed towards a tree.

'Oi, you crooked thief,' shouted Ammaji in rage, now turning around and shouting and chasing after the ape. 'Give them back. They're of no use to you, you stupid donkey.'

'Stupid *monkey*, maji,' said Hungry Hop, stopping in mid-track, stunned at her mistaking such vastly different animals for each other. 'He's a monkey, not a donkey.'

'Munkey-dunkey,' shouted Ammaji. 'Don't just stand there. Go after him.'

And remembering his duties, the Hungry Hop boy went at the creature, screaming and yelling, waving two sticks in such an alarming manner that even this dreadful monkey, disgusted at finding no peanuts, and a little intimidated,

dropped the cone, raced over the roofs of the shops and disappeared. The Hungry Hop boy retrieved the dentures
from a melting pool of chocolate and delivered them, carefully balanced on the end of a stick, to Ammaji.

Pinky could not remember being so mortified in all her
life. There she was, looking like a sweeper woman, with her
grandmother's dentures being displayed in public, first
atop an ice-cream cone being borne away by a monkey, and
then dangling humiliatingly on the end of a stick. What a
spectacle they had made of themselves. A cheering crowd
had gathered to watch the fun. But the Hungry Hop boy
treated the whole occasion with a nonchalance that made
Pinky weak with thankfulness.

'Here you are,' he said cheerfully and gave the stick a
shake. 'We have had enough exercise for a week, hm?' He
smiled such a nice white smile and then turned to bow to
the crowd, who shouted their congratulations. 'Of course,
after seeing you,' he said, turning back to Pinky, 'this monkey had to follow. He must have thought you were a long-
lost relative.' He laughed appreciatively at his own joke,
winking at Pinky to show he did not mean his remark to be
taken seriously. And – who can explain such things? –
Pinky, who had seen the Hungry Hop boy every week of
her life, had stopped on almost every trip to the market to
buy ice cream and thought nothing of it, felt her heart fall
for the second time in the day, as if from a cliff: Boom! into
wide empty space.

This Hungry Hop boy was kind. He was not embarrassed in the least. Nor was he ugly, after all. His hair was
curly and his nose was endearingly crooked, as was his
mouth. To think she had seen him so often, beautifully
dressed, and hardly noticed him at all . . . and today, here
she was, staring at him with new-found interest, wearing

an old white salwar kameez, badly cut and faded, with no nose ring, no toe ring, slippers without a trim or a puff, her eyes without the kohl that made them smoulder . . . So conscious of her drabness was she, she could not even manage to return his smile; in fact, it was all she could do to keep from bursting into tears.

And as soon as she was home, she *did* burst into tears. She cried tears of rage because she had looked so plain, because it was all her family's fault; she cried loud and long . . . Oh, she thought, her awful, awful father, who sent her out like a servant when other fathers went to all sorts of efforts to make sure their daughters looked well cared for and were properly dressed. Her horrible grandmother, who had added to her humiliation. Her terrible, terrible family, who would no doubt ruin all her chances of love for ever.

Oh, and she thought again of the Hungry Hop boy, who might, had she looked her usual self, have played a role in her life well beyond the mere parameters of ice cream.

She howled and howled, the noise so piercing and mournful it rose up into the leaves to Sampath and made his hair stand on end. Down below, Ammaji's mouth fell open at a particularly loud yowl, only to have her dentures fall out again – this time into the cooking pot.

'What are you crying about?' inquired Ammaji solicitously as she fished around for the dentures that were bobbing about in the gravy, being dyed a startling and permanent curried yellow. She lifted them out with a spoon and popped them back into her mouth. Surely it had been a very successful day?

Pinky wailed again. 'Ooh, hooo, hooo,' she answered despairingly.

Maybe she was just crying for the sadness of the world, thought Ammaji. 'Look at my teeth,' and she showed

Pinky, in an attempt to cheer her up, a fierce curry grin.

Stunned by the bright yellow, Pinky stopped for a moment.

'Oh, well, at my age what does it matter?' said Ammaji, pleased by her granddaughter's reaction. She sucked the flavour of their dinner from her teeth. 'Yellow teeth, blue teeth, black teeth, it is better than no teeth at all, isn't it?'

But Pinky, seeing how Ammaji was attempting to trick her from her tears, returned to her crying with a vengeance. 'Ooo, hooo, hoo,' she bawled.

10

By the time a month had passed, Mr Chawla had made all sorts of improvements to his family's living arrangements in the orchard, for, after all, they had been forced to relocate to rural surroundings and were unused to doing without town comforts – and why should they have to? He had tapped the hospital electricity lines for light with the help of the electrician, trailing a mess of wires leading from the electricity poles directly to the orchard. Courtesy of the excellent hospital supply, he spared them from all the breakdowns and fluctuations suffered by the rest of the town. He had also directed a whole slew of regular orchard visitors in laying a network of water pipes leading from an appropriate hole they had made in one of the main water pipes one dark night into a private water tank. Provisions such as matches, kerosene, candles and soap were delivered to him from the shop in town as a special courtesy, though they lived far out of the radius within which deliveries were usually made. Of these accomplishments, Mr Chawla was extremely proud.

Water gushed into the water tank all day long. In the evenings, a string of coloured lights decorated the paths in the orchard, dramatically illuminating the foliage and casting their soft light upon the family relaxing upon their cots in front of the watchman's shed. Over this shed there was now proper roofing of corrugated tin instead of just thatch, and inside there was a television and a tin trunk full of warm quilts and shawls. Soon, perhaps, he would be able to build an extension to their residence with a kitchen and a bathroom. He would buy a refrigerator and a scooter. True, Sampath had brought in no dowry, but Mr Chawla was not one to sit around and complain.

'Everybody can make something from nothing,' he intoned beneath the tree, for he liked to think that Sampath still appreciated and learned from his old father. 'If you try hard enough, something will work out. You yourself know how –'

'– a potter makes a pot from a lump of mud. A painter paints with camel's urine. A beggar holds out his empty hand,' said Sampath, finishing his sentence in such a glib manner Mr Chawla was a little taken aback at his son's cheekiness, but he repeated his point. 'The thing is to make do with what you have, even if it is nothing.'

But was there nothing? He looked up at Sampath, watched his face, thought of what he had said and felt slightly unsettled . . .

Then, after a while, he did not listen or look too closely any more. He rented out their old house in Shahkot to a secretary from the fertilizer company. He opened a new bank account and approached businesses in the area that might be interested in advertising about the orchard, a place that would not only ensure their products a large audience but also endow them with a sanitized glow of purity. And he began to think of stocks and shares. Stocks and shares were a good idea because they were not in the least ostentatious and Mr Chawla realized, when he saw the respect for the austerity of Sampath's life that visitors displayed, that he must keep a careful balance between the look of abstemiousness and actual comfort.

Perhaps the family should do without the refrigerator and motor scooter? Even the advertising? Oh no! Perhaps the bank account should be opened in the name of a special fund for building a temple? That way attention would be diverted to religious matters and donations would pour in. Not that he planned to embezzle and steal. They *would* build a temple! Then there would be even more donations. Endlessly, his mind bounded from scheme to enchanting scheme.

He obtained cuts from the scooter rickshaw men and the bus drivers to enter and park in the compound, and they were glad to oblige, for they themselves were doing a colossally good business by charging a flat fee for the round trip from the bazaar up to the orchard and back. Even buses thundering up the highways en route to farther destinations began making regular detours for their passengers to view the famous Baba in his treetop hermitage, the sweetness of his smile, the vacant peace of his gaze.

The path to Sampath's tree had been widened and was kept swept clean and sprinkled with rose-water; a small ladder had been set against the trunk so those interested in asking for blessing (and everybody was interested, of course) could climb up to the spot where Sampath dangled his legs. With his toes placed reverently upon their heads, they would claim his blessing and descend feeling smug and rather proud.

Other arrangements had been provided too. Ammaji had been put in sole charge of a tea stall operating from under a bit of canvas sheeting attached to four poles, and consequently she was able to spend her time chatting to her heart's content with visitors who ordered a snack or two, a Campa Cola, or even a light lunch to complete the pleasure of their outing.

Near the tea stall, Mr Chawla managed a small cart. Here, while also keeping his eye on everything else, he sold flower garlands, fruit and incense to those inclined towards leaving offerings for Sampath. This was a very nice system, because although he had to buy the supplies from the bazaar, he was given a large discount (after all, he was the father of the Shahkot hermit). These items he sold at a large profit, and then, in another lucky financial twist, the family reclaimed many of the coconuts and sweetmeats from the bottom of Sampath's tree at the end of the day to pile them back upon the cart so they could be sold once more the next day.

Sampath looked down at his charming visitors.

'Why are there so many opinions about the nature of God?' asked a disguised spy from the Atheist Society (AS) and a member of the Branch to Uncover Fraudulent Holy Men (BUFHM). 'Some say he has form. Others say he is formless. Why all this controversy?'

'The city inspector makes a journey to see a river,' answered unsuspecting Sampath, 'but he goes right at the time of the monsoon. He comes home and says the river is an enormous sheet of water with very high waves. Many months later, his aunty makes the same trip. She comes home and says: "Sadly my nephew is a bit of an idiot. The river is nothing but a dirty little drain." At the height of the summer a neighbour makes the same trip and says: "That whole family is unintelligent. The river is nothing but a dry stretch of mud."'

'Can anybody comprehend all there is to know about God?' asked someone else.

'Once you have broken the bottle you can no longer distinguish the air inside from the air outside.'

'Baba, can you talk about the problem of religious unrest in our country?'

'Haven't you heard a mother-in-law shouting at her daughter-in-law: "Is this the way to prepare dal?" Of course she thinks her way is best. But north, south, east and west, everyone eats lentils in some form or another and everybody receives their nutritional benefits.'

'I try to interest my children in spiritual matters, but they turn a deaf ear.'

'There is no sign of the fruit when you buy the shoot. A watermelon does not exist unless it is the watermelon season. Before you cut it open you should always put your ear to the rind while tapping on the side. In this way you can make sure it will be completely ripe.'

The spy made notes in a school notebook and scratched his head dubiously. This was his first important mission since he had joined the society that boasted of such distinguished members as the man who had revealed the mechanism that gave rise to the electric-shock guru, the woman who had uncovered the exploding-toilet scam, the clerk who had hidden himself in a vat of sweetened curd to overhear a conversation that led to the indictment of the BMW guru for everything from money-laundering and tax fraud to murder by poison. In fact, it had been a lucky thing the clerk had not eaten any of that curd.

The spy was determined that he too would thus distinguish himself. He was lonely in Shahkot; his village was far away and he was as yet unmarried. He hated his job as a teacher at the public school, hated the boys who drew unflattering portraits of him in their notebooks and pulled faces behind his back. Often he gave them exercises to do and escaped to the staff room, where he sat staring out of the window and smoking cigarettes. One day he would show the world; he would rise above his poverty-stricken childhood, the hovel he had grown up in with eleven brothers and sisters, his drunken and drugged father, his worn-out mother. One day the world would turn its attention to him at last. Applause. Prizes. Newspaper reporters. He would hold his face out to the light and, in the midst of adulation, discover his poise, discussing fluently and with the seriousness of an intellectual on television his opinion of things. 'Well, you know, liberation, as I comprehend it, comes from freeing yourself from the tawdry grasp of superstition. This is not a simple matter, you understand, for it is embroiled in historical issues, in issues of poverty and illiteracy.' Yes, his life had been hard. But he would overcome.

'What should I do, sir?' he ventured once more. 'I do not know what path I should take. I do not know what questions to ask. In fact, I do not even know what I want.'

'A child cries for its mother's milk, doesn't it?'

'I do not understand.'

'A baby bird cries for an insect.'

'But, sir . . . milk and insects?'

'A mother knows what its child wants and recognizes her child from the noises it makes. Consequently, you will be quite all right if you stop asking questions and wait for your mother to come to you. Be patient.'

'But –' he persisted. 'But, sir –'

Sampath's head began to buzz. What on earth was this man being so annoying for? He looked out into the leafy avenues about him and gazed moodily into the distance.

The spy from the Atheist Society looked happier. Clearly Sampath was at a loss for a reply to his clever questioning and was trying hard to avoid him. He went behind a tree and made more top-secret notes in his school notebook.

'Avoids questioning by pretending otherworldliness. Unable to discuss deeper matters of philosophy.'

Below Sampath the hallowed silence grew until Ammaji became uncomfortable with the quiet so loud and so big. 'Oh,' she said, 'sometimes his mind leaves the earthly plane. Don't be offended.'

It had not occurred to anybody to be offended.

'I myself have seen many holy men like this,' said Lakshmiji. 'Sometimes they sit completely still. Nothing can move them. They are like a bird on her eggs. Sometimes, though, they are frivolous and laugh, leap and dance. Yes, they can be like a child or a madman. Other times, instructing others, they return to the plane of consciousness to share their wisdom.'

'Yes, it is the face of a vijnani, no ordinary countenance at all. Look, just look at his face.'

Sampath's normal usual face! Pinky listened with astonishment to the things she was hearing.

'Oh,' said Ammaji, chiming in delightedly as she rolled a betel leaf, 'he was born with spiritual tendencies. Everybody was saying maybe he is a little mad, maybe he is a little simple-minded, but it is just that he could never interest himself in the material world. One time I gave him five rupees to pay the milkman and the next thing I heard was the milkman shouting: "Oi, ji. Look, ji, what your grandson has done." There was a strong breeze that day and while the milkman was measuring the milk, he had made a boat out of the bill and floated it into the canister. And hai hai, when it came to school what a terrible time we had. All the time: fail in Hindi, fail in Sanskrit, fail in mathematics, fail in history. Never could he concentrate on his studies.'

'Ah! For one like him, it is hard to keep the mind on such

petty and mundane matters. He will look out of the window and everywhere there is the glory of God.'

'It is true,' said Ammaji. 'I cannot tell you what a terrible time we have been having. It is very hard for a family. There we would be begging him: "Please study a little; at least pass; we are not asking for any miracles." But he would continue as he was, sitting for hours, looking at a flower, staring at the sky . . .'

'I knew of a sadhu from Rishikesh,' said a schoolteacher who had travelled all the way from Chittagong, 'who every day would emerge from his hut, look at a hot spring and meditate. He never practised any other austerities or study. Just the sight of the hot spring would send him into samadhi.'

'Oh, what terrible trouble we had in the post office.' Miss Jyotsna, who had become a regular visitor, was happy to claim intimacy with Sampath's formative years. 'Sometimes he would make an attempt, but we all said better not to do anything. Better let one of us do it or else there will be such a mess, we will never be able to sort it out.'

'And such a pretty girl we found for him!' said Ammaji, getting more and more carried away. 'But no, he would have nothing to do with her . . .'

'What use can a hermit have for ladies? For such a person, it is an affront even to suggest marriage.'

At this everyone nodded their heads. In that moment they too would like to be sitting like this, clean and pure, in such pleasant surroundings without their husbands and wives and extended families. How beautiful the Himalayan foothills were! How bountiful and lush! Butterflies fluttered through the landscape, tree pies and flycatchers flew from tree to tree, lizards sunned themselves on the tin roof of the watchman's shed, sliding down in a stupor during the warm afternoon, and the breeze rustled the leaves. Here and there were sprinklings of wild flowers, flowers with the colour and fragrance of fruit; flowers with gaping mouths and tongues that left the devotees tiger-striped with pollen as they passed by; that waved their anthers and brandished their stamens, that sent such scents up into the air, nobody could help lowering their noses into their fragrant petals.

Quietly, but in a sure, pleasant voice, Miss Jyotsna began to sing:

'There are footprints entering my house, but I have no visitors.
There is the sound of music in the trees, but the wind is still.
There are fingerprints over all my belongings,
But they don't match those of anyone in this household!
O Lord,
This hide and seek
Would tire even a patient man.'

How pretty she is, thought Sampath, looking down. He had always found her pretty. She was sweet too and had a beautiful voice. Eyes closed, swaying from side to side, she seemed genuinely lost in the words that flew from her small, round, ruby mouth. In a while, he joined her, all the devotees chiming in one by one. They had a wonderful time singing together.

How could he fool all these people? wondered the spy from the Atheist Society peeping out from behind the tree. What hold did he have upon them? What was it about him? He sniffed the air. The scent of cardamom and cloves wreathed up into the leaves from a cooking pot some-where. Cardamom and cloves and . . . what else? He sniffed again. The smell entered his nostrils and wormed its way into his brain. Yes . . . he sniffed. Something else . . . He made some more notes in his book.

In the mouse-hole-sized room he rented in a house full of lodgers, he drew up a plan for his investigation of the case that included research into Sampath's past and a list of all the basic information he should know about his suspect: when he slept, whom he talked to, what he ate and drank.

Then the spy remembered the mysterious smell in the orchard that day. A whiff of it still clung to his skin and clothes.

Could Sampath be drugged?

What had been cooking in that pot?

No doubt he was smoking ganja – it grew wild all over the hillside. But perhaps he was taking opium as well? And who knew what else?

The spy thought late into the night.

11

Far on a hillside roamed the lady responsible for Sampath's nutrition, a tiny figure on the crest of the university research forest, disappearing and reappearing among the trees, emerging at the point where the forest bordered the fields so as to check the cane traps she had set for pheasants and other wildfowl. They lived in the forest but ate from the grain crops and were as fat and delicious as wildfowl could be. When she spotted one in the trap, she pounced upon it and, without flinching, wrung its neck with a grip of iron. The profusion of greenery and space exhilarated her. And while it reduced her son to a happy stupor, it incited her to a frenzy of exploration.

Making her way into the deepest parts of the woods, losing herself amidst the bamboo groves, the sal forests, the towering moss-laden trees, she climbed higher and higher, taking paths made by goats foraging about the steepest slopes, barely wide enough for her small feet.

'Beware of the wild cats,' said the goat herders she met, surprised at seeing this delicate-looking town woman out alone in the forest. 'Beware of the snakes, the scorpions and leeches.' But she didn't care. She waded out into the muddy ponds to collect lotus stems, raided bird's nests, prised open tightly sealed pods, nibbled at the grasses and buds, dug at roots, shook the fruit from the trees and returned home with her hair wild, her muddy hands full of flowers, her mouth blue and red from all she had sampled. The corners of her sari were tied into knots containing ginger lilies and rain-fever mushrooms, samples of seeds and bits of bark. Sometimes she brought back a partridge or a jungle quail, strung on to a stick and carried over her shoulder. She returned via the steep path that led to the back of the watchman's shed so as to avoid the visitors and the talk which had ceased to interest her.

In the tin-covered porch Mr Chawla had constructed at the rear of the house she had set up her outdoor kitchen, spilling over into a grassy patch of ground. Here rows of pickle jars matured in the sun like an army balanced upon the stone wall; roots lay, tortured and contorted, upon a cot as they dried; and tiny wild fruit, scorned by all but the birds, lay cut open, displaying purple-stained hearts. Ginger was buried underground so as to keep it fresh; lemon and pumpkin dried on the roof; all manner of things fermented in tightly sealed tins; chilli peppers and curry leaves hung from the branches of a tree, and so did buffalo curd, dripping from a cloth on its way to becoming paneer.

Newly strong with muscles, wiry and tough despite her slenderness, Kulfi sliced and pounded, ground and smashed, cut and chopped in a chaos of ingredients and dishes. 'Cumin, quail, mustard seeds, pomelo rind,' she muttered as she cooked. 'Fennel, coriander, sour mango. Pandanus flour, lichen and perfumed kewra. Colocassia leaves, custard apple, winter melon, bitter gourd. Khas root, sandalwood, ash gourd, fenugreek greens. Snake-gourd, banana flowers, spider leaf, lotus root . . .'

She was producing meals so intricate, they were cooked sometimes with a hundred ingredients, balanced precariously within a complicated and delicate mesh of spices – marvellous triumphs of the complex and delicate art of seasoning. A single grain of one thing, a bud of another, a moist fingertip dipped lightly into a small vial and then into the bubbling pot; a thimble full, a matchbox full, a coconut shell full of dark crimson and deep violet, of dusty yellow spice, the entire concoction simmered sometimes for a day or two on coals that emitted only a glimmer of faint heat or that roared like a furnace as she fanned them with a palm leaf. The meats were beaten to silk, so spiced and fragrant they clouded the senses; the sauces were full of strange hints and dark undercurrents, leaving you on firm ground one moment, dragging you under the next. There were dishes with an aftertaste that exploded upon you and left you gasping a whole half-hour after you'd eaten them. Some that were delicate, with a haunting flavour that teased like the memory of something you'd once known but could no longer put your finger on.

Pickled limes stuffed with cardamom and cumin, crepuscular creatures simmered upon the wood of a scented tree, small river fish baked in green coconuts, rice steamed with nasturtium flowers in the pale hollow of a bamboo stem, mushrooms red- and yellow-gilled, polka-dotted and striped. Desire filled Sampath as he waited for his meals. Spice-laden clouds billowed forth and the clashing cymbals of pots and pans declared the glory of the meal to come, scaring the birds from the trees about him. Kulfi served her son with an anxious look, watched his face like a barometer. Turning blissful lips to the sky, or at other times looking down in pain, with tears pouring from his eyes, his ears exploding, barely able to breathe, Sampath would beg: 'More! Please, some more.' And triumphantly Kulfi would rush back to get another helping.

'You will poison him,' said Mr Chawla, genuinely worried when she embarked upon these efforts at a new cuisine. She would manage to ruin their fortunes entirely. 'If it were not for the family name, straight away I would take you to the mental home,' he mumbled. As the years passed, he found he understood her less and less instead of more and more. What went on in her mind? he found himself wondering sometimes. Did she think like a human being? He saw expressions of anxiety, of happiness, of peaceful-ness upon her face, it was true, but was she *considering* how she felt, analysing and reasoning?

'I have fed the food to a chicken beforehand to make sure it is not poisonous,' she assured him.

One chicken after another had been named the official taster to Sampath. When one keeled over and died, from natural causes or tainted food, a new one was kept tethered in its place.

So Sampath was safe and he made sure nothing would change when it came to his food; whenever he heard his father muttering about other cooking arrangements, he threatened to go on hunger strike. He had never eaten so well in all his life! His growing plumpness proved how well the meals agreed with him. Pink-cheeked and in an injured tone, as if he were being done out of his birthright, he said: 'Every son knows there is no cooking like his mother's cooking.'

The devotees, watching jealously, had begun to think that perhaps there was cooking unlike their mother's cook-ing. Previously, they had merely wondered at what Sam-path was given to eat, but as Kulfi became more and more ambitious, more and more sure of what she was doing, just one whiff was enough to send them wild. Far from consign-ing her to a mental home, they hovered about her greedily, trying to peer into the bubbling pots, to draw their fingers through the piles of spices on the grinding stone. But she shooed them away fiercely. 'Not for you, not for you,' she declared regally, and they backed away from the authority of her voice, the dignity of her bearing, and shook their heads, wondering what was the matter with them. Charging down the mother of the hermit! What had come over them?

'Baba, why are we so aggressive and greedy sometimes, when at other times we are just happy to sit beneath your tree?'

'On a hot day the bee buzzes louder, on a rainy day it sits quietly in its hive,' answered Sampath.

Though he wrote down everything he heard religiously, the spy had given up trying to understand Sampath. The more he saw, the more he was convinced that the secret of Sampath's presence, his odd words and antics, would be found in Kulfi's cooking pot. More determined than all the rest, he tried again and again to sneak past her in an attempt to collect a sample of her food in a bottle he had provided himself with.

But each time, as if she had been forewarned, Kulfi caught sight of the spy just in time and cracked him over the head with a broom. You could get yourself killed in the BUFHM, he thought, and watched from the bushes as she continued her work, slicing vegetables with vigour, beheading chickens and geese with nonchalant blows of her hatchet. But still, the more his efforts were thwarted, the more suspicious he became. The minute her back was turned again, he could not help but make one more attempt . . .

What with all the trouble Sampath's meals were causing, Mr Chawla decided to allow visitors only between the hours of lunch and dinner, between half-past noon and half-past eight in the evenings.

With limited access, the popularity of Sampath and his hermit-like reputation grew. However, the trick of limited access could not be applied when the monkeys arrived.

12

'Look,' Pinky yelled one day soon after the visiting hours had been put into effect. 'It is one and the same monkey who chased us in the bazaar.'

'Look,' chortled Sampath from his superior look-out position, 'a whole band of them!'

'That monkey is following me,' Pinky shrieked. 'Everywhere I go, it goes.' She turned to glare at her brother. 'Why are you so happy to see them?'

How could he not be happy? A whole cluster of interested silver-fringed black faces peered at him prettily from between the leaves of the neighbouring tree.

'Haven't I told you, Pinky, nobody is following you,' said Mr Chawla yet one more time.

But what did he know of the nasty qualities of these monkeys?

'Wait and see,' said Ammaji, showing a warning flash of lurid yellow between her lips. 'There will be trouble. You can see it in their faces.'

Kulfi slapped some wet clay on to a bird pierced with cloves and threw it into the open fire to cook. The air filled with smoke.

'Wait and see,' repeated Ammaji darkly.

And it was not long before the troupe from Shahkot, presided over by the Cinema Monkey, became regular visitors to the fields and forests surrounding the orchard. They rarely ventured out of town and people wondered why they'd made this trip up the hillside – had even the ape community obtained news of Sampath and organized a visit?

The monkeys, when they first arrived, looked upon Sampath, the strange sedentary member of another species they had spotted up in their usual domain, with some trepidation and maintained a wary distance, baring their grotesque and discoloured teeth, pulling faces, chattering in a scornful show of contempt and derision. Unbothered by their mocking, glad of yet another distraction, Sampath turned their dirty game right back on them and hooted and howled. 'Hoo hoo,' he cried, rolling his eyes, puffing out his cheeks in a way that seemed to cause mutual satisfaction, for these antics continued and soon the monkeys drew closer, extended their dirty wizened palms and nudged Sampath, at first gingerly, to see how he would react, and then with a great rude push once they decided he was not a threat. And how he could contort his face! A look of being very impressed showed across their monkey faces.

They looked even more impressed when they had spent long enough in the orchard to identify Sampath as the nucleus of this bountiful community they had come upon. Funnily enough, all the food in the orchard seemed clustered about this hooting boy who possessed qualities that, though not admired in them, seemed to be greatly appreciated in him. No doubt, the closer a human was to a monkey, the more presents he was given: the freshest fruit, the best nuts, were brought to Sampath's feet. He was not merely accepted, then, but endowed with elevated status within the monkey hierarchy. Through him they could receive the tastiest titbits. Before he knew what was happening, he was sharing his string cot with the cinema bully himself. Propped up simian-style against each other's backs, they awaited visitors in this their shared state of splendour, for no longer did the troupe spend its time scavenging in the market, stealing from the shopkeepers, terrorizing the likes of Miss Jyotsna and Pinky. Why would they do that, when they had realized soon enough that they could obtain their meals much more easily by sitting near Sampath and receiving the kind people who drove up for the express reason, it appeared, of bringing peanuts and bananas?

Fondly, the lady monkeys groomed Sampath as he sat, secretly pleased but shouting, 'Ow, don't pull my hair like that,' and swatting them. But, with amused, sly faces that looked as if they understood he was playing a little game, they circled back after being chased away to continue their attendance upon his glossy and shining locks, which, to their credit, grew even shinier and glossier with their care. Sampath enjoyed this attention more and more as he became used to the occasional tug or scratch.

'Look at that,' said Miss Jyotsna, who, like Pinky, had let out a shriek when she first identified the ape who had humiliated her at the cinema. 'Clearly he has charmed the monkeys.'

They sat grouped about Sampath like a silver-haired and graceful bodyguard, yawning and scratching at their beautiful selves. Almost all the ladies had a story, second-if not first-hand, of torn saris and petticoats, and they marvelled: 'Look at that monkey. Gentle as anything! The Baba has subdued the beasts.' A priest visiting from the church in Allahabad was reminded, he said, of St Francis of Assisi, who was always depicted so touchingly surrounded by creatures of the forest.

The behaviour of the monkeys was just another procla-
mation of Sampath's authenticity. 'Think of all those shams,'
said Miss Jyotsna, 'all those crooks posing in their saffron,
those gurus who are as corrupt as politicians . . .'

Oh, they gloated, their Baba was not like that. He was an
endless source of wonder. He had even cast his spell upon
the wild beasts of the market.

'Hmph,' snorted the spy, who was, to tell the truth, a little unsettled by this new occurrence. 'No doubt it is just
well-developed human–monkey interaction,' he said.

'Human–monkey interaction,' said Miss Jyotsna, highly
offended by this disrespect being paid to her old colleague.
'Go ahead, brother, you try your hand at human–monkey
interaction and get sent to hospital covered with monkey
bites.'

But though some of the visitors were happier about the
monkeys' arrival, seeing Sampath's effect upon them, Mr
Chawla thought his mother's instinct had been accurate
right from the start and he mourned his clever trick of selling and reselling the offerings provided by the visitors.
Those greedy monkeys ate everything they could grab and
run away with.

Kulfi grew worried about her kitchen and began to store
her things away more carefully.

And Pinky, too, unelated by this onslaught of apes, was
reminded of the insuperable Kwality Hungry Hop boy
every time she saw them and consequently, several times a
day, she burst into hysterical tears.

Ever since her encounter with the Hungry Hop boy over the
denture affair in the bazaar, Pinky had gained a new feeling
of compassion for her brother. This was not a feeling she had
ever had before; it was different from the exasperation or

amusement she had usually experienced in relation to him. But one morning she had looked up at his feet dangling from the cot and realized that they must surely have hit upon a similar vein in the state of things. No doubt, weighed by the same concern with fragility, inevitability and doom, Sampath had been driven up into the branches, away from this painful world. She remembered his face as he was going to school, how he would always try to climb up on to the roof to be alone when he came home, and she felt terrible about how she had harangued him, shouting up the stairs . . . Now, she felt, she too understood the dreadfulness of life, recognized the need to be by herself with sadness, and from this moment of realization onwards, she spent hours sitting under Sampath's tree, in a private cocoon within which she indulged her every thought, wrapping herself in endless imaginings, endless ruminations, snapping in quite an uncharacteristic way if she was interrupted.

And then, down in the bazaar, there was the Hungry Hop boy, who did not even know of the misery she was going through. 'Baap re!' she concluded, he certainly ought to know, for it was a very awful and upsetting way to feel. This was an unbearable state of affairs. Here she was, no longer her own strong self and without anything else that might be of some consolation. Suddenly angry, she began, once again, stormily, to cry. And while she was crying over the Hungry Hop boy, she was simultaneously horrified that her own mind could create such a terrible cage, and she longed for the freedom of her earlier life, wished she could catch hold of this dreadful boy, throw him down the hill-side, stamp on him and hit him with a stick.

'What should I do?' she asked her brother, as he sat high above her clucking his tongue at her tears while also examining the green veins of his arm, the woodiness of his heel. 'I am going crazy,' said Pinky. 'I feel like a firework that has been lit by a match.'

'If a firecracker has been lit,' said Sampath, 'then it is going to explode, like it or not. Unless you throw it into a bucket of water. And then, what a waste of a firecracker.' He looked at his arm, the mahogany of his skin. He watched the sun's watermark upon his belly, its rise and fall through the leaves.

Pinky decided her brother was quite right. There was no reason for her to drown herself in a bucket of tears, and neither would she sit and suffer through feeling like some faulty firework, with all the sparks flying inside her instead of blazoning outwards in a display that would surely create some sort of effect, make some sort of an explosion. And an explosion, she knew, is never without a certain amount of satisfaction.

The next morning, filled with resolve, she changed her clothes, painted her face, waited for the time when her family was distracted by the commotion of Sampath's daily bath and made her escape up the path that led from behind the shed. She had painted her eyes thickly and blackly about the upper and lower eyelids, and pinned a bunch of flowers to bloom like detonations over each ear. Like an actress ready for a performance, she was prepared. Her lips pressed tightly together, earrings swinging from her unusually small earlobes, she strode down the path towards the bus stop, breaking the branches that threatened to bar her way, kicking the stones from the path, despite her flimsy slippers and delicate, unprotected toes.

The spy, barred from Kulfi's cooking pots by the new visiting hours, had been loitering about outside the orchard, trying to think up an excuse that would allow him in anyway, when he saw Pinky on her way to the bus stop. He decided to kill the time before he could be legally admitted into the orchard by following Pinky instead, just this once, just to make sure there was nothing more going on there than an ordinary trip to the bazaar . . .

Here and there she caught a glimpse of him ducking, always just a little too late, behind bushes and tree trunks. But for once she was not bothered, although she noted with satisfaction that her father was certainly wrong: men *were* following her. On she strode. She climbed on to the bus and, when he did as well, she speared around her ruthlessly with her hairpin, giving the spy such a jab he was forced to rush straight to Dr Banerjee for a tetanus shot when they reached the bazaar.

It was still early. The smoke from the fires that were being started in the tea stalls obscured the pale winter sun. The Hungry Hop boy stood in the grey bazaar with all the shopkeepers, who were only just getting ready to open their stores, yawning and scratching at their bellies meanwhile.

By any standards this boy was rather slow. He had some humour, it was true, and was well-meaning and good-tempered for the most part, but he was not very conscious of what was happening in the world about him. Until the Cinema Monkey had begun to forage elsewhere, he had considered it part of his daily duties to chase him away. Thus he had not thought twice about his rescue of Ammaji's dentures, and neither had he realized that now Pinky's ice-cream buying was a significant ice-cream buying as opposed to an insignificant ice-cream buying. The various times she had endeavoured to bump into him in the street had not affected him in the least, for again he often bumped into her in the street. As impervious to Pinky's charms as always, he had continued upon his way, his life rock-solid and unbothered by love. When the right time came, the right girl would be found for him without the disruption of romance. In the meantime, he enjoyed himself singing along to love songs on the radio and pinching and poking the odd girl on the bus who happened to catch his eye.

Thus it came as quite a surprise when Pinky changed her oblique strategies in a direct demand for recognition. He looked at her amazed as she bore down upon him dressed in the colours of battle, dark with kohl, mouth like a stab wound, storming through the bazaar as if at the head of the conquering army. 'Enough,' she muttered, 'quite enough.'

She walked up to the Hungry Hop boy, who was removing the bit of corrugated metal propped against the opening of the van.

'What, you want to eat ice cream this early in the morning? Clearly living in the mountains is getting to your brain,' he said, smiling.

Seeing him she was filled with a rush of elation and rage. How placid and smiling he was! For a minute she thought she might kiss him, but the vein of aggression pounded powerfully within her and she bit him instead. She bit his ear so hard that the Hungry Hop boy shouted out and his voice boomeranged about the town.

He was being hurt. He was being murdered. 'Ai. Yai. Yai.' The black and white polka-dots of her sari swam alarmingly before his eyes.

People came running from every direction. 'What happened? What happened?'

A piece of his ear lay upon the ground.

Women who were preparing lunch boxes and getting the

children ready for school opened the windows and leaned out. Forced to leave his breakfast because of all the ruckus, the Superintendent of Police, who had been sitting at the tea stall, arrived. 'Arre! What is happening here?'

The Hungry Hop boy held on to his maimed ear and yelled, 'She attacked me, sir, she attacked me.'

Pinky was marched, trembling, glowering, to the police station. She had drawn blood before, in the school play-ground. She spat out the salt taste of it. The pour of red from Hungry Hop was like the spill of passion and pain. She trembled, but if there was any fear in her she refused to show it or to let it get the upper hand. Or even to admit it to herself. Her courage rising, she walked dignified, behind the superintendent. Meanwhile, the Hungry Hop boy, trem-bling more violently than her by far, his courage ebbing with each passing moment, was taken to the family clinic, his ear packed in a tub of vanilla ice cream that had been handily obtained from the van to keep it frozen so that Dr Banerjee might sew it back on.

'Human bites,' said Dr Banerjee, relaxing at the door to his clinic, talking to the local newspaper representative after seeing off both the spy and the Hungry Hop boy, 'are most common in the summer and winter season, but can occur all year round. They are more common in the morning than in the afternoon. Indeed, although people concern them-selves more with animal bites, human bites should be given close attention, for human mouths contain up to forty-two species of bacteria. Thus they can be more dangerous even than spiders or dogs.'

'Since when do ladies in the town bite gentlemen?' the policeman asked of Pinky, fierce and seemingly unrepen-tant, smouldering upon a bench back at the police station.

'You will end up in the mental home if you persist in demonstrating that that is where you belong.'

But she looked at him unvanquished. She was not one to be frightened by such threats. After all, this very asylum had been brought up several times in relation to her mother and her brother and, losing its ominous quality, it had begun to sound like a rather familial sort of institution.

'This is a serious matter,' the police superintendent said, waving his baton up and down. 'Really very serious.' He was happy at having such an interesting thing to do for a change. 'Yes, you have created quite a to-do here.'

At this moment one of the other policemen came and whispered something urgently to him.

'What?' he said. 'Are you the sister of the man who sits up in the tree? The Baba is your brother?'

She nodded sulkily.

The superintendent went out of the room and then came back with several curious policemen. 'I'm sorry,' he said. 'We did not know your family name. Please come along with us. We will escort you back to your family.' And he gave a sniggering policeman, overcome by the humour of the situation, an unpleasant shove from behind. Didn't he know he should be careful? The police were not going to upset the family of one of the town's most respected personages. 'In Shahkot, we honour and respect our hermits,' he said.

Still glowering, Pinky was driven back to the Chawla compound in the station jeep, accompanied by the superintendent and several other policemen. She was glad she had bitten Hungry Hop.

The policemen all climbed up the ladder to receive Sampath's blessings. The superintendent placed his unpleasantly greasy head under Sampath's toes and felt as though he were being bathed in pure holiness, as if he were being washed gently and cleansed in sweet blessing; it reminded him of the feeling he had when he was given presents on festival days. 'Can you tell me, Baba, when can I expect a son?' he whispered.

Sampath, not in the mood to answer, withdrew his foot and tucked it under him. He was a little afraid of policemen, who had more than once shouted at him as he ignored the traffic rules when bicycling to work at the post office.

'No need to worry,' said Mr Chawla hurriedly, not wishing to upset the police. 'You can ask him another time. Sometimes it is hard to get him to pay attention to what is happening down below.' Why did Sampath always behave badly just when important people came to visit?

But the policeman nodded amiably. 'People like this are not of this world and so it is natural that sometimes they separate out.'

Sampath opened one eye like an owl so he could maintain his distance, while also joining in this interesting talk about separating out that had just come up: 'If you keep muddy, churned-up water still, soon the dirt will settle to the bottom. If you churn up milk, the cream will rise to the top. Ponder the nature of what lies within you and behave accordingly.'

'Can we have a photograph, sir?' the policemen asked, awed. 'For the police station, sir.'

The monkeys entertained themselves by throwing peanuts at the policemen's heads.

Mr Chawla had not even thought of photographs! What a market he was missing. He hitched a ride into Shahkot on one of the scooter rickshaws that were constantly coming and going, and brought the town photographer back with him. The photographer climbed up into the tree with several cameras and a painted piece of canvas depicting background scenes on both sides. On one side there was a scene of swans floating in a pond with many pink lotus flowers; on the other, a magenta sunset over the sea with a far boatman stalled at the horizon in a tiny boat.

'Helloji,' said Sampath, delighted at the photo opportunity. 'Aren't you the boy who sent secret love letters to that girl from the convent school?'

The poor photographer was so taken aback, he dropped his equipment bag.

'Don't pay any attention,' said Mr Chawla soothingly. 'Somehow he knows these things. But please don't worry, I won't tell anyone.'

Still, despite Mr Chawla's kind words, it took the photographer several minutes to recover himself and gather strength enough to climb back into the tree. Along with Mr Chawla, he positioned the canvas sheeting behind Sampath and, hanging treacherously from the branches, he did his best to find the ideal angle of Sampath's face, first against the sinking sun and then amidst the lotus flowers.

When the monkeys, who were pulling the leaves off a neighbouring tree, spotted this invasion of their territory, just like that, in broad daylight if you please, they let out screams of outrage and bounded back into the tree to help Sampath defend their domain. Leaping from branch to branch in a state of red-gummed, brown-toothed indignation, they almost caused the already jittery photographer to fall down upon his head.

'Sorry, sir,' said the poor young photographer, new to the job. 'I cannot do this. My mother would not like me doing such dangerous work.'

'No, no,' soothed Mr Chawla. 'It is perfectly safe. I myself will talk to your mother if you wish. Look, we will make it safer right away.'

Ammaji was stationed down below with a pile of stones and a slingshot made of a branched twig and a piece of black elastic. As she sent the pebbles flying, keeping the irate monkeys at bay, the photo shoot was completed according to the specifications of Mr Chawla. Sampath had wished to pose properly with a nice smile and perhaps an arm thrown casually around a branch. But his father had not allowed him to do any such thing. 'Keep your hands folded in your lap. Keep a gentle smile upon your face,' he instructed. 'No showing of your teeth.'

'No charge,' said the rattled photographer, happy just to get out without having been bitten or hit with stones. 'The Baba's blessings are enough for me. It is for the honour of my family name to do this. And please, sir, do not tell anybody about those letters . . .'

The photographs of Sampath were printed in hundreds of sheets by the Kwick Photo Shop at no cost and were cut into little squares by their tea boy.

'How handsome my grandson is,' said Ammaji when she saw the photograph of Sampath sitting cross-legged amidst lotus blossoms, his umbrella askew, his cot at a slant, looking distracted because of all the commotion with the monkeys and pebbles and the photographer dangling before him with peculiar, militaristic and medical-looking gadgets.

'It is a terrible picture,' said Pinky. 'He has not even combed his hair. You can see the birthmark on his cheek. And he is wearing nothing but his undershorts. How can you say it is a good picture?' A good picture was one where a man posed with perfectly oiled and coiffed hair, with a nice tight shirt and nice tight trousers, sitting on a moped.

But anyway, despite Pinky's disapproval, these pictures

were sold from Mr Chawla's cart and proved to be very popular. Soon they made their appearance everywhere, permeating the shops and houses of Shahkot and travelling much farther afield.

In February, this picture was even printed in the *Times of India*, together with the headline 'The Baba of Shahkot in his Tree Abode'. *This peaceful orchard outside Shahkot, it read, has been transformed by a glut of visitors rushing to see the hermit of Shahkot, whose rare simplicity and profound wisdom are bringing solace and hope to many who are disheartened by these complicated and corrupt times. 'There is a spiritual atmosphere here that I have not seen anywhere else in India,' Miss Jyotsna, a postal worker, told this reporter. She professes herself a frequent visitor to this hermit, whom disciples affectionately call 'Monkey Baba' or 'Tree Baba' in reference to his fondness for animals and the simplicity of his dwelling place. While admitting all who come to see him, he limits the hours when he is available to protect his secluded lifestyle . . .*

After the appearance of this article, letters by the thousand began to arrive for Sampath from all over the country. Mostly they bore no address, just the photograph of Sampath in his tree pasted trustfully upon the envelope. Inside were pleas for help and questions from ardent wisdom-seekers galore.

Delighted by this excuse to visit the orchard even during work hours, Miss Jyotsna from the post office took to making regular trips in a scooter rickshaw to deliver these enormous quantities of mail, while Mr Gupta sulked back in Shahkot, for he had decided he did not like it when he was not the centre of attention.

At the annual meeting of the Atheist Society in a neighbouring town, the spy addressed his colleagues. 'Did you see the newspaper article about the Chawla case? It is completely outrageous. Even the press in this country goes along with this rubbish. In fact, they are the ones who propagate it. They take a rumour and put it into official language and of course everybody who reads it promptly swallows it as the whole truth. This madman belongs in a lunatic asylum and just look at how everybody is running to him bringing him presents.'

He went on for so long and in such an impassioned way, it grew past dinner time for many people in the audience. One member leaned over and spoke into the ear of another: 'He is going a bit overboard, don't you think? Why is *he* so upset by all of this?'

But the spy now felt personally involved and personally outraged, and continued upon his tirade for yet another hour. It was precisely people like Sampath who obstructed the progress of this nation, keeping honest, educated people like him in the backwaters along with them. They ate away at these striving, intelligent souls, they ate away at progress and smothered anybody who tried to make a stand against the vast uneducated hordes, swelling and growing towards the biggest population of idiots in the world. Even minuscule little countries like Taiwan and the Philippines were forging ahead. If he had any sense, he would leave this blighted country and emigrate. But no, he had chosen to stay back and do his bit to change things, even though he had once been knifed in the arm with a metal hairpin by the sister of the Baba for this sacrifice. Who could tell what permanent effect this would have on him?

He began an additional elaboration upon his suspicions of what Sampath was being fed, how his food was so carefully guarded nobody was allowed near, how he might be drugged, his spirits raised or lowered to abnormal levels, the spy was not sure which. He talked of how he was going about his research regarding this topic, of the book on hallucinatory substances he had procured . . .

The roars from the stomachs of the audience rose to a deafening level. Really, this man was too much. Talking of food when they should all be sitting down to their own nice hot dinners that very minute.

'Did he say he was stuck in the arm with a hairpin?' asked the member of the audience who had been restless an hour and a half ago. 'Or was it in the head? He is quite right, though, it has had a severe effect on him.' And this time the man did not talk in a whisper, but as loudly as he could. 'Oh, sir,' he shouted directly at the spy, 'don't you think your time is up?'

The spy was interrupted midstream. For a second he was thrown off balance. 'Before the mosquitoes are killed the night is uncomfortable,' he replied.

'Well, that is certainly true,' said some other individual.

'Thank you,' said the spy. 'Once you open a bottle of soda water, you should drink it before it goes flat.' But the blood rushed to the spy's face. Without thinking, he was repeating things he had heard under the Baba's tree. And now he was taking credit for it! He didn't have the courage not to.

Later, he tossed and turned in bed.

What did he want in his life?

The emptiness that stretched like the black night about him made him all the more determined to expose Sampath as a fraud.

13

One afternoon, about a month after their first appearance in the orchard, the monkeys found five bottles of rum while rifling through the bag of a man who had stopped to see Sampath on his way to a wedding. They drank it all up and that afternoon, when they resurfaced in Sampath's tree, where they were accustomed to joining him for a little siesta at 3.00, they felt unable to slip into the general state of stupor that overtook the orchard like a spell particular to this time of day.

Sampath stretched out drowsily upon his string cot. He held his hands up so their shadow fell upon the illuminated trunk in front of him and he watched his fingers move, creating a lotus blossom with petals curling and uncurling, a swimming fish, a lurching camel. He was amazed at the sophistication of the shapes he made. He let his fingers wriggle like a spider to scuttle across the impromptu stage of the sun-stamped tree. These scuttling insect legs caused a shiver to course down his spine and he shook his hands as if to get rid of a spider inside him. He remembered the way he had sometimes scared himself in their home in Shahkot, flicking his tongue in and out in front of the mirror – a snake's tongue, not his own. He thought of human beings with bird-beak noses, people with swan necks, cow eyes, bird-heart terror or a dolphin's love for the ocean. People with sea-water tears, with bark-coloured skin, with stem waists and flower poise, with fuzzy-leaf ears and petal-soft mouths. He closed his eyes and tried to sleep. The Chawla family and various visitors, including the spy and Miss Jyotsna, lay scattered throughout the orchard. But the monkeys refused to settle down.

'Do keep quiet,' said Sampath sleepily. 'You are making me nervous with all your jumping.'

But, pulling faces and hooting, they leapt about the tree and carpeted the ground below with twiggy flotsam.

'Stop this,' said the spy, who was hit with a little twig. He was trying to think through his thoughts and put them all in order, since they had become so jumbled lately.

'Yes, keep quiet,' shouted several other devotees. There was something truly wrong with these monkeys.

'They are acting very strangely,' said Mr Chawla.

'Perhaps it is the full moon,' said Ammaji.

But when Mr Chawla discovered the empty rum bottles near the outhouse, it became apparent that it was not the moon at all.

'Oh, they are only monkeys.' Sampath felt compelled to defend them. 'What can they possibly know? When the rest of the household is sleeping, the child puffs on his father's hookah.'

'It is true,' said some, while others, embarrassed that alcohol had been discovered on the compound, just giggled. 'It is not the monkeys' fault. Always men are the degenerate ones. It is very sad, but in a place like, this with so many visitors, you are bound to get the bad with the good. Isn't that so, Babaji?'

'First a chikoo is raw,' said Sampath, 'then, if you do not pick and eat it quickly, it will soon rot and turn to alcohol.'

What was he saying? That the time of perfection passes, that you should eat a chikoo at the right time only, that everything is part of nature, that good becomes bad or that bad is not really bad because it is all part of the nature of a chikoo? Oh, sometimes he was hard to understand.

One thing, however, became clearer by the day: the monkeys had developed an unquenchable taste for liquor. Bam! How they loved it! In an immediate and explosive way that must surely have been made inevitable by the forces of destiny. Who knew if the scientific community has determined the addictive properties of alcohol on the langur or not? The truth was plain to see. They loved it in a crazy, passionate way; they began to forage with a new recklessness that made people wonder if they had not gone a little mad. Peanuts and bananas didn't mean a thing to them now.

A few days after their first encounter with alcohol, they discovered a case of beer in a delivery van. A week later, a bottle of whisky in a rickshaw. Then more beer. Then more rum.

Dark faces full of determination, wild, liquid eyes, they ran with great leaping strides to meet each bus that arrived, each scooter rickshaw that drove up, searching for liquor of any sort, inspired, no doubt, by the memory of a certain race to the blood, a mysterious lift to the spirits. They grew bolder and bolder, rifling through the contents of bedrolls, grabbing hold of shopping bags and chasing away the owners, who ran off screaming in horror. It was as if all their old bazaar habits were resurfacing; as if, bored by plenty, they were doing their best to re-create the excitement of their former life of thievery and assault in the midst of public outcry.

When they were chased from their shameless attempt at plunder, they bared their teeth, so the travellers retreated for fear of being bitten. When the pilgrims shook their fists at them, they shook their fists back and jeered loudly. As soon as they were clapped and shooed from one place, they appeared doing something worse in another. It was like warfare. They mimicked the pilgrims and lined up along with them by Sampath's tree, smacking each other with glee as they waited for his blessing.

It soon became clear that the display of affection between Sampath and the monkeys would not extend to include everybody within its charmed circle; that their simian charms, so dear to him, would not endear them to anybody else. Peanut-laden film-lovers might be making their way to the cinema unmolested, but evidently the monkey problem had merely shifted focus.

Concern permeated the devotees' happiness. Almost overnight, it seemed, they had a new problem on their hands.

'If they were a nuisance before, it was more in the way children are naughty,' said Miss Jyotsna sadly to the others as she watched the monkeys raid her bag of mail, scattering the letters in a frenzy of disappointment when they discovered no bottles in her possession.

'Yes,' agreed one gentleman. 'In fact, they were endearing in their very naughtiness,' and though he had gone too far, everyone sympathized, for generally speaking there was some truth to what he said.

14

One afternoon, a little while after the frequency of these unfortunate events had accelerated, Mr Chawla stood thinking under Sampath's tree. The monkeys were getting more and more out of hand and he had a unsettling feeling that their hallowed days in the orchard might be under serious risk of disruption.

But the family bank account in the State Bank of India was growing by leaps and bounds and he was eager to buy shares in the VIP Hosiery Products company; they could do without a disturbance to upset this nice little venture he had set to sail. He looked to the right and left, surveyed their domain with its paths and a little arrow pointing in Sampath's direction, with its advertisements that hung colourfully on the neighbouring trees: Dr Sood's Dental Centre, Gentleman Tailors – 'God made Man, we make Gentleman' – for Campa Cola, Limca, Fanta and Goldspot, Ayurvedic Talcum Powder and Odomos Mosquito Repellent. All paid for by lavish donations, boxes of nuts and more sweetmeats, yellow, green, pink and white, than anybody knew what to do with. If it was not for Mr Chawla none of this would exist. None of it.

'Sampath,' said his father, 'perhaps it is time to build you a proper hermitage. The problem of the monkeys is getting out of hand. If you lived inside a concrete structure, we could keep them out and control things. Anyway, we can't have you sitting in a tree for ever. What will happen when the monsoon comes? There are only a few months left now.' He envisioned a whole complex with a temple and dormitory accommodation for travellers designed to suit modern tastes in comfort, a complex that would be a prize pilgrimage stop and an environment he could keep control of.

Sampath looked at his father. Could he be hearing correctly?

Seeing Sampath's face, Mr Chawla was filled with irritation. What a ridiculous look of overdone incredulity! 'And you had better start learning some philosophy and religion,' he said. 'People will soon get tired if you cannot converse on a deeper level. I will buy you a copy of the Vedas. You really cannot sit saying silly things for ever.'

The monkeys threw apples at Mr Chawla's head for fun, though it looked as if they were attempting to protect Sampath. He gestured angrily at them, but they greeted his protest with a barrage of bananas. Mr Chawla lost his temper.

'They are making a mockery of us,' he said, his sense of dignity hurt. 'It is getting too much. People will think you are a circus act. Sitting in the tree with drunken monkeys! We must put you in a proper building immediately.'

'I am not going to live anywhere but in this tree,' said Sampath. 'And the monkeys are not drunk right now. They are only playing.'

When his father had gone he realized his heart was thumping. He could not get the horrible thought out of his mind. Leave his tree? Never. Never ever, he thought, his body trembling with indignation. Fiercely, he studied the branch in front of him. He and his father were as different as black from white, as chickens from potatoes, as peas from buckets. What did he think? Did he think he would just climb down and return to his old existence like some old fool? He had left Shahkot in order to be alone. And what had they all done? They had followed him.

He spotted a beetle crawling out of an aberration in the bark right beneath his very nose. Covered in brilliant green armour, antlers sprouting from its head, wisps of wings like transparent petticoats peeping ridiculously from beneath its hard-shelled exterior; it seemed a visual proof of the silliness of his father's proposition. Gradually, he calmed down. How beautiful these insects around him were, how incredibly beautiful: huge, generous flowery butterflies, bees with tongues that he could see hanging thin and long from their mouths, finely powdered beetles with kohl-rimmed eyes and clown-faced caterpillars with round noses, false beards and foolish feet; creatures made from leaves and sepals, petals and pollen dust. He watched an endless parade of them, wriggling, hopping, flying by, emerging as if from the bubbling pots of a magician, with the flicker and jewelled shine of . . . of what? Of the essence of wind and grass? Of sunlight and water?

When his mother brought his dinner to load on to the pulley system, Sampath peered down at her. 'You know,' he said, 'they are planning to build a hermitage, but I will not leave this tree.'

Kulfi looked up at him. Of course he could not leave. 'We could always poison them, you know,' she said, trying to comfort him.

And he smiled, despite himself, to think of the time he had been rushed, vomiting and blue, into the emergency room at the Government Medical Institute after eating a meal she had cooked. Joyfully, he had missed a whole week of school. Looking at her he felt a pang of tenderness. His mother, the monkeys and himself, he thought, they were a band together.

'You had better change your ways,' he warned the monkeys. 'There will be trouble for all of us if you don't behave better.'

But the monkeys did not behave better. In fact, they behaved a good deal worse.

About a month after their first encounter with alcohol, apparently disgusted by their meagre success in the orchard, the langurs made a trip to the bazaar, where they overpowered the old woman who sold illicit liquor from a cart. They devoured her entire supply and, drunk as could be, drunker than ever before, they returned to the Chawla compound.

'Keep away,' Sampath shouted at them when he saw them approaching. 'Keep away until you're sober.'

He knew there would be trouble. But they did not heed his warning. Exuding the rough, raw scent of local brew, they arrived like hooligans and, in true hooligan style, proceeded to turn everything they could upside-down.

Sampath had seen drunks every now and then, of course, but only once had he had a direct experience with one, when he had found himself in conversation with the neighbourhood drunkard outside the tea stall. Tottering about, crashing into the tables, the drunk had embraced Sampath, who was the only person there. 'Say you are my best friend,' he had pleaded, clutching hold of Sampath. 'Are you my best friend?'

Sampath had been scared to death. 'Yes,' he had said.

And the man had embraced him. 'Everything I have is yours.'

But I want nothing that is yours, Sampath had silently pleaded. The man had smelt of a sewer filth that had turned Sampath's stomach. His eyes had been red, his breath powerful and he had held Sampath as if he would never ever let him go. Finally the man was chased away by the tea-stall owner, who came outside to pelt him with stones. Sampath had cycled far away and stood in middle of a field to recover. Still as the plants about him, gulping in the quiet and greenery.

Oh, but the monkeys were different, he thought, despite himself, as he watched them raid his mother's kitchen, overturning pots and pans, sending buckets rolling through the orchard, the discordant clatter of metal filling the air. They were so beautiful, so full of graceful strength. Tails held high above their heads, they knocked over the milk can so the milk disappeared into the grass. They tore open the sacks of supplies that were piled under the porch, and the rice and lentils spilled into rivers of gold and green, black and white. They ate quantities of raisins and nuts, almonds, cashews and tiny, precious pine kernels whose theft caused Kulfi to chase after them with her broom. But they avoided her easily, as they did all the intrepid devotees who had formed a whole pebble-slinging army under Ammaji's jurisdiction – bravely, they sent their stone artillery flying from slingshots, running back and forth through the trees, feeling rather drunk themselves on the excitement of it all.

'Don't touch the monkeys,' Mr Chawla yelled, waving his arms, trying to snatch slingshots from the hands of the devotees. 'They are dangerous. In this state, they will turn on you.' But at present even he was unsure of exactly what to do. He should have taken precautions. He should have nipped the problem in the bud. But how?

When they had become bored of the kitchen, they tore newspapers to shreds; they stole Ammaji's comb and lodged it high in a branch, they broke the spokes of Sampath's umbrella and left it battered and full of holes. They pulled the washing from the lantana bushes where it was laid to dry. As Pinky shook a leafy branch – 'You badmashes. Go back to the jungle where you belong' – they loped about in circles, half draped in garments, dragging saris and sheets and petticoats behind them, tearing the fabric to shreds, strewing her finery like paint over the tree tops.

By now, the greater number of devotees had relinquished their slingshots and retreated down the hillside, frightened by the langurs' growing violence, worried that they would be chased and robbed and perhaps even bitten.

Sampath's tree thrashed in a fierce chaos of branches and leaves. In it, he was tossed here and there, and upside-down. What was happening? It was all too quick for him to take in. His heart leaping and falling, skipping and jumping, his mind in a whirl, he was sure if he let go he would be sent careening through the air to land, concussed, upon the ground. Before his eyes a sickening blur moved and shook.

'Come down, Sampath,' everyone shouted, but he held tightly on to his cot.

'If you are not going to come down, keep absolutely still,' his father yelled. 'Do not move.'

Caught up in this drunken dance, savage faces, long tails, saris draped in purple and yellow streamers all about him, useless bits of thought flew past Sampath, everything going by too fast for him to stop and grab at them. He could jump; but no, it would be his undoing. He could pull on the monkeys' tails; no, he would shout. No, he had better hold tight . . .

Luckily, before anybody was actually bitten or hurt, the monkeys bounded off into the university research forest, tired of the noise people were making, or perhaps tired of the orchard, their wild spirits carrying them farther and farther to the opposite hill, where the family could see them continuing their onslaught upon the meek landscape, wrecking every tree, uprooting every bush, expending their energy on anything that came in their way, leaving entire areas of the forest ravaged as if by a tornado.

Before dawn the next day, Mr Chawla was up and dressed, making his way into town as fast as he was able. Worry knit his brow. Things had gone too far. After all, diseases like rabies were carried by these animals. Something would have to be done. The old District Collector had just left and the new one had not yet arrived. There was no top authority for him to visit, but he decided to see all the other officials he could think of to make it clear that it was their responsibility to do something about this disruption to sanctity and peace in Shahkot.

15

It was about six in the morning and already the Shahkot newspaper man was delivering the story all over town. It arrived with a thwack upon verandas and porches, against doors and through windows.

Soon, the newspaper man bicycled by the house of the Chief Medical Officer, who sat in a wicker chair on his veranda in happy anticipation of the paper and the cup of tea he had just poured out to steam gently and fragrantly before him. Now, this newspaper deliverer was somebody who prided himself on his perfect aim and, seeing the CMO sitting quietly there on the veranda, he attempted to deliver the paper right at his feet. It arrived like a missile, zipping through the air and landing with a crash into the tea tray.

'Really, you are too zealous,' shouted the CMO after the figure bicycling quickly away, and he settled down sadly to the day's news without his usual comforting cup of Darjeeling. 'Rama Rama Rama Rama Rama,' he muttered as he read of the monkeys' exploits and he rubbed his feet together to encourage himself in the face of such bothersome news. 'Rama Rama Rama Rama Rama.' He mulled things over. This would be trouble. He knew it. It always meant trouble. It was precisely this sort of thing that caused his ulcers to get worse.

He lived in a constant state of panic that his ulcers would

get worse, and everybody knew that nothing was worse for ulcers than worry and this worried him all the more. He moaned and rubbed his feet. He would have to go on a strict herbal diet right away. Fenugreek sprouts and onion juice. Onion juice and more onion juice. Oh, he wouldn't be able to bear all the onion juice he'd have to drink.

He had not even given the matter at hand a proper thought, or decided on an appropriate response to this ruckus, when he heard the sound of Mr Chawla arriving in the cycle rickshaw he had taken all the way down the hillside. The residence of the Chief Medical Officer happened to be first on the road between the orchard and Shahkot. The CMO looked up surprised as the rickshaw, having gathered the momentum of a slight slope to the north of the bungalow, swept in front of his veranda with a loud squealing of brakes.

Mr Chawla leapt from his seat on to the gravel patch in front of the veranda steps and ran up them to stand threateningly in front of the official, disregarding the muddy footprints he left on the polished, red-painted floor.

Without stopping for any pleasantries, he began to shout. 'Have you heard the news?' he almost screamed in his high state of excitement. 'The monkeys are threatening my son. They are threatening the ladies of the community and disturbing the peace. They are destroying the religious atmosphere of the whole compound. We must have them removed without delay.'

The Chief Medical Officer was taken aback by this vehemence. What was he to say? He had been unfairly caught at home in his pyjama kurta. This was disastrous for a person with a sensitive nature like his. First the newspaper man and now this crazy fellow. He looked desperately at the patches of butter-yellow sun upon the lawn still mostly composed of shadow. It was ridiculous for him to be the CMO when he himself was sick.

'My respected friend,' he said finally, thinking of the trouble that could come about if things were not left well alone, 'you must remember that ever since the monkeys' association with our beloved god Rama, these animals are hallowed with special affection in our sacred tradition. They have their own devoted supporters.' He looked around again. 'Myself included,' he said as firmly as he could, hoping Mr Chawla would leave so he could return his mind to the subject of his stomach and give orders to his servant for onion juice to be prepared. But when Mr Chawla opened his mouth to start talking again, he lifted up the telephone receiver. 'I will call the head of the biology department at the Lady Chatterjee University. As you perhaps know, Vermaji is an expert in human–langur interaction and maybe he will have some peaceful ideas on how to defuse this situation. Of course,' he said after dialling the number, 'the line is busy as usual, or else it is not working.' And he tried again.

'Isn't he the same person,' said Mr Chawla, 'who set baits filled with sleeping pills to contain the problem at Ranchi? They did not catch even a single monkey. These animals are very street-smart. They have learned all sorts of tricks in the bazaar.'

The man they were trying to reach was at that moment studying the morning papers with great interest. *Monkeys cause menace in holy man's retreat. Last night drunken monkeys went on a wild rampage, causing people to flee the scene*, he read with unnatural delight. 'No doubt this is not the last we shall hear of this,' he said to his wife, seated across the table from him. 'You know,' he went on jubilantly, 'perhaps I will have a chance to try out my new hypothesis. If the leader of the group is killed and hung in full view of the other monkeys, they might disband and disappear into the forest . . . Of course, they might also just elect another head monkey . . .'

He was very fond of theories. Something had only to catch his attention and, regardless of whether it was a problem or not, he immediately had a hypothesis, complete with steps to be taken and possible conclusions. This trait was of great annoyance to his wife. Should she be drying dishes, he would creep up from behind and watch her with his shiny eyes. 'You know,' he would tell her. 'I'm sure if you carried the dishes outside the sun would be hot enough to evaporate the water in as much time as it takes you to dry the plates. In conclusion, if the hypothesis proves true, you will save energy and time.'

But what about the time and energy it would take her to carry out the dishes and spread them upon the balcony? She was infuriated. Or would he carry them out for her? All his theories, in her opinion, were worth nothing. She remembered the time, years ago, in the terrible summer of drought, when he had invented a fan to draw monsoon clouds into Shahkot. And the last time he had tackled the monkey problem, he had had to concede complete failure. The monkeys had not eaten a bite of the sleeping-pill-laden food; hungry street urchins had gobbled it down instead, and then promptly fallen into a deep sleep that lasted, in one case, up to forty-eight hours. It had caused a terrible uproar among the slum dwellers . . . Not that this disaster had dampened her husband's zeal, of course. Here he was with yet another idea that would cause trouble for a lot of people and end in nothing.

'Disband?' said his wife. 'The monkeys will probably attack you instead, and if they don't, all the Hanuman Monkey Temple people will, and you will be khitchri,' she announced with satisfaction.

Really, his wife had a bizarre sense of humour, one with rather a vicious edge, he thought. She had no scientific training at all, but apparently had no inhibitions about attacking his every thought with childish retorts. This is what he got for sharing his intellectual pursuits with her. Sighing, he picked up the telephone to call the CMO, who might perhaps be able to give him some more information on the monkeys' misdeeds.

Way off in the local army outpost on the edge of town, the commotion of the morning continued. The Brigadier, who had just finished with the papers, picked up the ringing telephone.

'Chief Medical Officerji?' said Verma.

'Wrong number,' said the Brigadier.

'Sorry,' said Verma.

A second later the phone rang again. 'Oh, sorry,' said Verma. 'You know how mixed up the telephone lines are in this town – only now and then do you get the right number.' A few minutes later: ring, ring.

'Will you stop phoning me?' shouted the Brigadier angrily.

Tring, tring. 'Oh, sorry, sir.'

The Brigadier slammed down the phone, unplugged it and retired to the bathroom, where he sat upon his Western-style toilet with his binoculars, looking carefully for any birds that might be about that morning. He was on an endless quest to raise the count of birds he spotted in the area: bird-watching soothed and relaxed him like nothing else in his regimented life. Cormorants, black storks, paddy birds, cattle egrets, little bustard quails; orioles, drongos, chestnut-bellied nuthatches; barbets and honey guides; parakeets and nightjars; flycatchers and hoopoes. The list went on and on, but it was his dream, more than anything, to be able to list the green pigeon in his bird-watching log-book; yes, the simple green pigeon, that had for so long been invisibly goading him with its song. Everywhere he went, the Brigadier carried his book with him so he might write down the name of each bird as he saw it, but he recorded most of his sightings from the bathroom window, which had the best view of all: over the valley and with a bank of fruit trees nearby. '*Treron phoenicoptera phoeni-coptera*,' he murmured to himself like a mantra.

But that morning not even a crow or a sparrow interrupted the unbroken expanse of sky. Disappointed, he lowered the binoculars and watched his soldiers going through their morning exercises on the parade ground instead. Hop. OneTwoThreeFour. Hop. FiveSixSevenEight. Hop. NineTenElevenTwelve. It was all very well, he reflected, thinking back to the morning's events, that his soldiers should hop and march, but what use was there for all this discipline?

Left, right. Left, right. Stand at ease.

What hope was there for the army? When the telephone system did not work and, he remembered the newspaper reports, when monkeys developed a taste for alcohol and went on the rampage?

He leaned out of the window, still on the toilet seat, with a megaphone, to shout: 'Double march. Jump to it.'

The soldiers, realizing they were being mysteriously observed from farther up the hillside, leapt like frogs and, in their confusion, scattered in all the wrong directions.

Somewhat mollified and feeling better about the day after

having shouted at his men, the Brigadier retired for his bath. He looked up the schedule that was mounted behind plastic on the wall by the water taps. 'Monday,' it read, 'back of the neck and ears. Tuesday, between the toes. Wednesday, the back,' and so on. Ah, it was his day of the week for washing behind his ears and neck. Each morning he paid attention to a different tricky part of the body. In this way, in seven days, every crease and crevice and difficult-to-remember spot was given a good scrub, despite water rationing. Of course, he washed his face every day.

But just as he was working up a good lather to apply to himself, he remembered the army mess, with its well-stocked bar, where he enjoyed a whisky soda almost every night. The monkeys must, at all costs, be kept away!

Rushing out of the bathroom in a way he knew he would later regret, he replugged his telephone and attempted to call the police superintendent, whose assistant answered and snapped: 'He has already gone on investigation,' which was untrue. The police superintendent could not be disturbed because he was at that moment getting his shoes shined at the shoe stand behind the station.

Aware that there was no point in calling the District Collector, for the new DC had not yet arrived at his posting, the Brigadier then tried to call the Public Health Department, but got instead a film star vacationing in the mountains, the Malabar Sweet Shop, the D'Souza household and the Patedar Shoe Store.

In frustration, the Brigadier took up his cane and, feeling grubby behind the ears, got into his jeep to visit the CMO. The CMO, despite a distinct pain in his side, had donned his Gandhi cap and set off along with Mr Chawla to see Verma of the university, albeit by a roundabout route that gave them the benefit of a good view of the mountains. Verma himself had left his house for his customary walk to the university through the Badshah Gardens with his friends Poncha of Epidemiology and Sinha of Virology.

Thus they all missed each other and that morning, anyway, the monkey menace was not discussed by the authorities.

'Oh, just look at how bad you've been,' said Sampath, when the monkeys reappeared in the orchard later that day.

Their dark faces peered from the battered foliage of the tree, looking contrite. Holding their heads, the distillation of pain and hardship in their expressions, they sat limply propped against whatever branches had not been wrecked and left to hang like the useless limbs of the war-wounded.

'Yes, you are very bad,' said Sampath. But he could not help but be charmed by them anew each time he saw them and he sounded like a fond parent trying hard to be disapproving. 'Of course you feel sick after all that. In fact, I myself feel a bit sick.' He forgave them completely. He could not blame his lovely monkeys. This was not their fault. It was the fault of those who brewed the liquor that had turned the langurs into alcoholics.

With grunts and burps, the monkeys suffered through what was probably a combination of indigestion and bad headaches.

16

In a room in his family's house in the bazaar, Hungry Hop sat nursing his ear, no longer throbbing and painful but adorned with small stitches to remind him of that very strange day in his life when he had been bitten by Pinky Chawla for no apparent reason. Since then, he had developed such a constant pounding in his heart, he had not yet mustered the courage to venture outside.

'Poor boy,' said his family, twelve women and three men, clucking their tongues beneath his room, looking upwards where, through the ceiling right above them, Hungry Hop sat by the window, fingering his ear for hour upon hour. 'He has really been given a scare. That crazy girl,' they said. 'It is best he stay inside and rest for a while longer. He never was a very strong boy.'

The days had gone by. The thought of Pinky went round and round Hungry Hop's head like a fish in a bowl; he could not get her out of his mind. He remembered those black eyes, that red determined mouth floating in the midst of billowing waves of polka-dots . . . the determination of that face! How terrifying!

Clearly, he had not taken his first brush with out-and-out danger in this world with very much spirit. And, as it transpired, his instincts in this matter were sadly to be trusted, for as he sat tearfully house-bound, his aggressor of old was plotting and planning yet another assault upon him.

'Once the rain has filled up all the holes in the earth,' Sampath said to Pinky as she sat morosely beneath the tree, 'a worm has no option but to emerge.'

He did his best to say something to his sister that would be helpful as well as acceptable to her, although he himself was fraught with worry over the fate of the langurs and, for that matter, his own fate. Already, of course, he had heard the first mumblings about modern hermitages and monsoon rains, and he could see exactly where it was all heading. And now that the monkeys had behaved so badly, he had no idea what was in store for him. Concrete hermitages! Phoof! A true hermit lived in a tree or on a rock, in a cave or a hole.

He looked down at the reflection cast by the morning sun upon the grass below: his own figure in its crazy contraption of tilted string cot and raggedy, monkey-battered umbrella, and the shadows of the monkeys grouped about him, their long tails hanging. Peaceful for once, full-bellied and quiet, they were in one of their most endearing moods; lazily, in perfect placid companionship, they regarded him and yawned. He thought that he would never be able to do without them. All the fun would disappear from his life: the teasing, the games, their naughty behaviour – their shamelessness and outrageous charm . . .

He looked at the tree that was such a good home. Its smooth, spacious branches of silvery tan that stretched wide and far-reaching in knotted, twisted curves and delicate bunches of spreading leaves. How important this had become to him. Here, sitting not too high and not too low, he had seen the world in absolute clarity for the first time, the days emerging as if purified from nights of a clean and brilliant blackness. The sunlight coming in through the leaves at daybreak, shifting and flickering, breathing its fire-breath upon the bark, falling now and then upon Sampath, whom it treated as if he were not the solid being that he was, scattering him like water . . . He felt weightless here, rocked by this lambent light, lapped by the swell of flower and grass, of leaves as rich as fruit, being warmed to their different scents. All about him the hills rose darkly up into a sky that stretched like a sea, white-stippled and warm, to the very rim of his eye.

How strangely it made him feel, Sampath thought, how strangely he thought of beauty. He was greedy for it, insatiably greedy. He could watch it constantly and never could he do it justice . . . At first, he had stared intently, watched everything about him with a fierce urge to take it all and imprint it within himself, every detail, every sweep. He had stared so that tremors ran over him, until this encounter with something that he could not believe, lying there right before his eyes, had him in its thrall. He had closed his eyes to check if it had indeed entered him, as he hoped it would – to see if the landscape before him could be conjured up inside him, at will.

But, again and again, he opened his eyes to find that no, the picture in his mind could not replicate what lay outside; he had only to turn to have it all rush away, the way the night's dreams recede like waves, leaving you with nothing when you wake. He could not claim it. If only it would reach out and claim him instead. If he stayed here long enough within reach of its sights and sounds, might it not enter him in the manner landscape enters everything that lives within it? Wouldn't the forest descend just this bit lower and swallow him into its wilderness, leaving his family, his devotees, to search fruitlessly for a path by which they might follow? He thought of the way the forest's army of weeds constantly invaded the grassy patch of the orchard, the way its insects, birds and monkeys interwove their lives with his. Of the way in which wind and rain wear down rock and smooth down stone, the way the calm of a sweep of hill can settle in the eye of one who stays long enough, still enough; how landscape rests everything within itself . . .

His thoughts were interrupted by the sound of Mr Chawla returning from town. Seeing his father's face, the face of a man filled with a mission, irritated, angry, but determined, Sampath was positive there was more trouble to be expected. And he knew from previous experience that when you dread something so very much, it often happens. Poor monkeys, he thought. Poor, poor monkeys . . . And poor, poor myself . . . What would happen now?

Down below, Pinky looked for pen and paper to compose a note. Although she was happy to have bitten Hungry Hop, she was desolate at how this appeared to have signalled the end of their long association. From childhood days we have known each other, she thought. It is not nice to suddenly withdraw over one small thing. When she was little, she had bought ice cream from Hungry Hop's father, who had been accompanied in those days by a small Hungry Hop. Later, when Hungry Hop himself had taken over the business, she had continued her patronage of their family van. She thought of what Sampath had said about worms being forced out by heavy rains and was heartened by it. No doubt if she barraged Hungry Hop with reminders of herself, hammered at his life in whatever way she found possible, flooded him with missives, he would have little option but to emerge and face her.

She put all her effort towards writing the note she had

decided to deliver to him. After several alterations, it read: 'I am so sorry to have bitten your ear. But it was done only out of affection. Please understand, the sight of you filled my heart with so much emotion, but it unfortunately came out in the wrong way. Here's wishing you a speedy recovery.'

She felt rather proud of her reserve and simple eloquence. She was giving vent to her feelings, she thought, albeit in a constrained, reasonable and amiable way. Certainly, she had reached a new level of personal development, a new pinnacle of maturity. She hoped this would convince Hungry Hop of her ultimate good sense and sanity, and pave the way for many further notes and encounters. With the piece of paper in her pocket, she departed for town.

She arrived at the Hungry Hop residence, still calm and filled with the influence of Sampath's wisdom. Although the men were out at work, the Kwality Boy was being kept closely guarded by the women of the family. They were all seated outside the entrance to their home, drying their hair in the sun after their once-a-week shampoo with soap nut. It looked like a good-tempered, leisurely family scene. They teased each other and painted each other's nails, passing around a plate of guavas with chilli and salt, but Pinky was aware that if she was spotted and identified, these women could transform themselves into a formidable army. Despite her own laudable abilities when it came to out-and-out warfare, she would be unable to defend herself against so many of them once they were aroused.

She slipped into the back alleyway. Didn't they know anything about family planning? Far too many women in that family, she thought with disgust as she made her way between the heaps of rubbish and scraps to see if she could catch sight of Hungry Hop from the rear of the house. And there – oh wonderful life! – looking wanly from the bath-room window, she saw his face.

Once more her spirits were caught up in their dervish-like tumble and her sense of calm, so solid a minute ago, vanished like vapour. The same compelling influence that had held her in its rabid rush the last time she had seen him in the bazaar engulfed her again. Helpless before it, know-ing she had to do something quick, she picked up a stone and, her nerves in a thrum of she knew not what emotion, she fastened her note to the stone with an elastic band from her hair and threw it, with deadly aim, straight at Hungry Hop, who was absorbed in staring dolefully out over the rooftops into an empty patch of sky.

He had not even noticed her presence in the alleyway down below and starting from this bullet that flew out of nowhere to hit him squarely on the jaw, he staggered back, dislodging as he did so the hair-oil bottle that had been bal-anced on the windowsill. He collapsed on to an upturned bucket against the wall. When he realized he was not dead and when the black sheet that appeared before his eyes as if to signal his end had disappeared altogether, he picked up the missile that had inflicted the painful blow. Shaking, he read the note that accompanied it.

An hour later, he sat still dazed upon the bucket, ponder-ing the strange possibilities of affection. Was this love? he wondered. Was it not love? How could it be? Was this a per-version, a malformation of the real thing? A trick?

Hammering at the door, his youngest sister shouted: 'Come on out. What are you doing in there?' She rattled at the door. 'Come on,' she said, banging. 'Hurry up. We need the oil.' Now that their hair was dry, she had been sent by the other eleven ladies to collect the hair-oil bottle; they were anxious to massage their heads with perfumed oil before embarking on the long and painstaking task of braiding it and arranging it into loops and buns.

Oh, but was this love?

The littlest sister had been joined by several older ones. Finally, they managed to open the door, by breaking the thin hook that held it closed, and discovered their brother still crouched down against the mildewed wall, but, though they searched and searched, the hair-oil bottle was nowhere to be found.

'What have you done with the hair-oil bottle?' they asked Hungry Hop, whose beautifully oiled and perfumed curls betrayed him as the last user of the product. They were terribly angry. The sight of the swelling on his jaw made them somehow even angrier. No doubt he had slipped while taking a bath and hurt himself. Their pathetic brother who had lost the hair oil, who was constantly getting injured or injuring himself. At first they had been patient and sympathetic, but there was a limit to these things after all, and his constant attempts to incite their pity were getting tiresome!

'Ooh, now you are really getting on our nerves,' they said in a quick about-turn of feeling.

'It is time to snap out of things,' said his mother. 'Find your backbone and pull yourself together.'

But, amazed by love, Hungry Hop looked right through their exasperated faces. Redolent with oil, he was still thinking about Pinky Chawla, who was likewise indulging herself in thoughts of him as she took a whiff from the bottle she had caught beneath his window.

The very next day she arrived in the back alleyway at exactly the same time and, catching sight of Hungry Hop again – for it was his regularly assigned bath hour – she threw him a rose. This time, Hungry Hop, his heart aflutter, succumbed to the mysterious compulsion welling up inside him and responded with his mother's hairnet. This incident marked an important change in their relationship: the beginning of a mutual involvement, a series of feverish exchanges that took place almost daily, with Pinky hovering about his house with some token of affection in her pocket and Hungry Hop waiting by the bathroom window. As the days went by, they managed to exchange all manner of bottles, toffees, sweetmeats, handkerchiefs and nightclothes. Also a comb, a toothbrush, an ear pick, a bar of soap, a pomegranate, some photographs and a towel.

Hungry Hop's sisters and aunts now forced to hammer regularly at the bathroom door, shouting: 'What are you doing in there?' realized quickly enough that something had gone very wrong. The bathroom was being emptied of supplies. Was Hungry Hop so depressed and troubled that he was spending hours flushing things down the toilet? But the toilet drain would not be able to take such a surfeit of offerings, and where was his jungle-print shirt that nobody could find?

When the truth came to light after a sister had spotted Hungry Hop throwing his mother's petticoat out of the window to his previous attacker, the family became crazy with worry. Clearly he had lost his stability. As if under a dangerous spell, his fear of Pinky Chawla had somehow been perverted into an unsavoury affection.

'Be careful,' they warned him. 'We will send you to your uncle in Dubai if this behaviour persists. We will marry you off immediately.'

It would be the end of their good name to be associated with Pinky. They had made some discreet inquiries and discovered what had happened to the family of Pinky's maternal grandfather when he fell under the spell of Kulfi's mother. That was the downfall of a fine family. And they were told it had all started in much the same manner. They began to make immediate inquiries about girls from normal, matter-of-fact, ordinary families. Who cared about dancing and cooking and high IQs? All they wanted was some sane steady girl. They whispered to the people who were on the look-out that they were willing to negotiate even in the matter of the dowry. This is how worried they were.

And they sent a message to Mr Chawla: 'Please keep your daughter from bothering our son.'

Mr Chawla confronted Pinky: 'What is this all about? You are always complaining that people are following you and now the truth comes out – you yourself are doing the following. That is that,' he said. 'You are not to associate with ice-cream vendors. A shopkeeper type! In fact, not even a shopkeeper type! An ice-cream-cart type. Our family name will be destroyed. You should set your sights higher than yourself, not lower.' How dismayed he would have been to find the ice-cream family making similar remarks about *his* family. He ordered Ammaji to accompany Pinky on her trips to town. He was far too busy with other matters to keep an eye on her himself.

Ammaji, however, did not much like this role of chaperon. At first, she did her best to run after Pinky and even donned special gym shoes for this event. Still, despite such arrangements, Pinky strode on far ahead.

'Do not go so fast,' Ammaji begged. 'Are you trying to outrun a Maruti jeep? I am too old for this. Look at your brother sitting quietly. None of this running around,' she panted. Finally, after three-quarters of an hour, she gave up and sat down to rest. To Pinky's satisfaction, thereafter, she settled in front of the grain store on all their trips to town, to talk to the other old ladies coming and going, and waited for her granddaughter to return from doing whatever pleased her. Then, they caught the bus back together and present a united front before Mr Chawla.

Thus the Hungry Hop women were forced to guard their Hungry Hop boy even more closely than they had done before, keeping a constant watch for Pinky, the stalker of their son, and they chased her with sticks, all twelve of them, the one time they caught sight of her. After all, they knew they could not go the police. Look at what had happened the day Pinky had bitten Hungry Hop. This girl was a sly and scheming witch. They kept a watch out of windows. They posted a permanent watchwoman in the back alleyway. All of the sisters and aunts were recruited to keep guard. It was lucky there were so many of them. It was always useful to have a large family, even if it was mostly girls . . .

Pinky was forced to retreat to an infuriatingly powerless position and she spent a few days in tears, until, that is, she hit upon the ancient idea of bribing the milkman to carry notes back and forth. In this wonderfully practical way, Hungry Hop and Pinky cultivated their romance and amazed their families by their good humour in the face of a situation that seemed, to others, to be not at all amusing.

17

Things had gone from bad to worse, and not many people in Shahkot were in the best of spirits these days. Sampath, shadowed by worry, attempted to write a poem.

He remembered, in his sadness, a singular day at the Mission School when a Brother John had taught them literature. Brother John had been dismissed after a week of teaching for pinching the bottom of the sweeper woman. But though he had departed in disgrace with a soiled reputation, Sampath remembered him as a being filled with beauty who had imparted to him his single inspired moment at school. While Sampath was indulging himself dipping his fingers one by one into the ink pot, his attention had suddenly been caught by the lines Brother John was reading aloud from a small volume in his hands. 'Poetry,' said Brother John, 'is born of hardship and suffering, of pain and doubt.' Then he proceeded to recite. 'All morning they have been calling you in,' he said, in such a way that Sampath was covered with goose bumps. 'Ten relatives to cook for and you're the girl. Their voices echo in jungle darkness, but no, don't answer. Stay by this shore. For what do they know of fin's fine gold rising to light in pale water?'

Sampath had felt very sorry for the girl with ten relatives. And: 'What do they know of fin's fine gold?' he repeated, trembling all over. Never again during his days at that terrible establishment had he felt touched like this.

Now he tried to compose something as well.

'But no, don't answer,' he said aloud. 'Stay in this tree. For what do they know of . . . of . . .' Of what? 'What do they know of . . . of the sun? What do they know of my tree? Of the monkey problem?' No . . . that didn't sound right. 'What do they know of . . . a grey donkey going to the market?' No, that wasn't a good line either. 'What do they know of . . .' Oh dear. He tried to think of some worthwhile thoughts to put in his poem. He thought of how the moon goes around the earth and the winter season comes after the monsoon. Of how years pass, leaving memories, and how the future is unknown, of how a man can speak while an animal cannot, and how people speak many languages and cannot understand each other. But try as he might, he could not break through to anything that seemed profound, or right to put in his poem. And what is more, these thoughts kept getting disrupted by the overwhelming concern of what was to happen to him and to his life in the orchard. 'What do they know . . .'

'What do *you* know?' he put his head down to ask of a red ant. 'What?' He raised his hands to the parrots. 'Will I be all right?' he asked out loud into the indifferent air.

The ant scurried by and the birds ignored him. And what did he himself know? Oh, he felt petulant; he should not have even begun. 'What do you know . . . What do you know . . .' It was to clear his mind he had climbed into a tree, not to befuddle it. Here he was thwarting his own ambitions.

As it was, only those who managed to enclose themselves in their own worlds and disregard the battles going on managed to sleep at night. One of these fortunate few was Kulfi, mother of the Monkey Baba himself, who had managed to brush away the entire furore with the langurs as if it were nothing but a minor annoyance of keeping her supplies locked up inside instead of out in the open, of having occasionally to chase a monkey with her broom. Preoccupied by her own thoughts, into which nothing else ever seemed to really penetrate, she continued on the path along which her life led her.

Doggedly, the spy followed. Thus far his research had led to nothing, and as if this lack of success were not enough, he was beginning to wonder if something in his constitution had been jiggled out of place. He was dismayed by how much space in his head had been taken up by Sampath's teachings. Ever since his lapse in the Atheist Society's meeting, he had been nervous about Sampath's influence upon him, and the more nervous he was, the more of Sampath's lines he discovered entangled inextricably with his thoughts. 'Wrestle not the sweet vendor's daughter.' He could not help but have it occur to him on all sorts of odd occasions. 'Spit not at the doctor's son. Why think about futter when you have plenty of butter? Don't say you like watermelon when someone gives you pumpkin. Don't eat a fiffle to save a piffle. Every plum has its own beginning. Every pea its own end.' With this sort of thing in his brain, he was finding it hard to follow his usual rational line of thought.

He was being seduced, he realized in a flash of terror. They were trying to brainwash him, using the equivalent of jingles and suave advertising. He had spent far too long in the orchard. In fact, to tell the truth, he had found he was enjoying his time there.

As soon as this thought occurred to him he was doubly terrified. He had better solve this case immediately and get out of the orchard as quickly as possible.

Keeping what he hoped was an unsuspicious distance,

the spy tried not to lose sight of Kulfi as she sometimes ambled, sometimes darted up the hillside, showing no more concern for following a path than a bee.

Kulfi was beginning to feel a little tired of what she had been finding in the forest. She looked under a rock, by a tulip tree, along a stream. She needed a new ingredient, she thought, sniffing the air, something exciting and fresh to inspire her to an undiscovered dish, a new invention. She looked up into the sky.

Already she had cooked a pigeon and a sparrow, a woodpecker, a hoopoe, a magpie, a shrike, an oriole, a Himalayan nightingale, a parrot . . . She had cooked a squirrel, a porcupine, a mongoose, all the wildfowl that could be found in those parts, the small fish in the stream, the round-shelled snails that crisscrossed the leaves with silver, the grasshoppers that leapt and jumped, landing with loud raindrop-like plops upon the foliage.

Diligently, she searched for a new plant, a new berry, a new mushroom or lichen, fungus or flower, but everything about her looked familiar and dull. No new scents enlivened the air and she wandered farther and farther away. As she wandered, she began to daydream.

She was the royal cook of a great kingdom, she imagined. There, in some old port city, ruthless hunters, reckless adventurers, fleets of ships and whole armies lay at her beck and call, were alert to her every command, her every whim. And sitting in a vast kitchen before an enormous globe, imperiously she ordered her supplies, sent out for spices from many seas away, from mountain ranges and deserts that lay beyond the horizon, for spices that existed only in the fantastical tales of sailors and soothsayers. She sent out for these and for plants that grew on islands no bigger than specks in the ocean, or on mountain peaks devoid of human habitation. She sent out for kingdoms to be ruined, for storehouses and fields to be plundered and ransacked. She asked for tiger meat and bear, Siberian goose and black buck. For turtles, terrapins, puff adders and seals. For armadillos, antelopes, zebras and whales. She demanded elephants, hippopotamuses, yaks and cranes, macaques and . . . monkeys! Monkeys! Oh, to cook a monkey!

Into the bamboo, past the green and yellow banana grove, out through the nettles, up to the hilltop. Exhausted and bedraggled, the spy gave up trying to follow her and climbed a tree from where he hoped to be able to keep up his watch. But, of course, he promptly lost sight of her altogether as she vanished around the curve of some rocks.

18

Far from being deterred by the public disapproval that had been expressed after their drunken orgy, the monkeys kept busy demonstrating how this was no isolated incident to be easily dismissed but, on the contrary, a whole new way of life for them.

Ammaji chased them from dawn till dark, assisted by her battalion that was sprinkled about the orchard, each person being allotted a daily ration of pebbles and a sling-shot made by herself out of sticks and lengths of inner tub-ing she had rescued from old tyres. Everywhere you looked there was someone running through the trees as if involved in an archaic exercise in weaponry, letting the pellets fly. But nowadays the monkeys merely shrugged them off, realizing they did not really hurt, and instead the devotees themselves suffered many injuries, what with stones flying backwards instead of forwards and hitting them in the face.

When the monkeys were not in the orchard or the bazaar, they took to waiting in the trees growing by the market road and accosting people on their way home from the bazaar in the hopes of finding a bottle of toddy or even rum. Leaving their victims in a mess of apples, ladyfingers, Postman oil and who knows what other supplies, they bounded away unconcerned about the damage they had caused, contented if they had been successful, but still on the look-out for other victims if they came away empty-handed. It became dangerous to walk through the area alone, and people who lived there organized special groups to go shopping together. They kept their windows and doors closed, saying their prayers as the monkeys bounded over their tin rooftops with a vast crashing sound of thunder. They tried never to be by themselves in any exposed location. Despite these precautions, in a sad event that took place in a private garden, two young men drinking to their success in the university examinations were bitten and taken to the local hospital with monkey-teeth marks upon their arms.

A monkey bite can prove to be as dangerous as a cobra bite in that monkeys often carry rabies, which can, of course, be as deadly as snake venom. Rabies is one of the worst illnesses a lady or gentleman can contract. It is more common in the summer than in the rainy season . . . With his usual dramatic flair, Dr Banerjee published a whole-page article in the next day's paper on the subject of monkey bites.

Immediately there was an uproar. Moaning in fear for his own safety, the Chief Medical Officer tried to do his duty and issued his own statement saying that as yet there was no problem with rabies, and under no circumstances should anybody succumb to panic-mongers and antisocial elements. They would persevere towards a working solution to this delicate problem.

Then, as if to undo any sense of calm that might result at this assurance, the Hanuman Temple took this opportunity to compose its own combative statement, officially joining the furore and expressing outrage at the indecent treatment of these monkeys. Clearly, forces bent on corrupting great Hindu traditions were at play, they said. They would sacrifice themselves for the religion's good name, if necessary.

Reading this, the Superintendent of Police, the Brigadier and every politician for miles around shook with renewed terror, realizing that they were in for a severe law-and-order problem of the worst religious degree.

'Some fruit must be eaten with the skin,' said Sampath.

'If you cannot find a car, you must do without.'

'If you do not find a bottle of rum, you will not drink a bottle of rum.'

'If your Auntyji finds a lump of silver, she might very well keep the lump of silver.'

'If your two-year-old son behaves badly, you will not think to exchange him for another. No, instead you will wait until he behaves better . . .'

But, he realized, he was losing the heart to carry on, and nobody was paying any real attention to what he said any more.

Below his tree, two fervent camps of devotees had been formed: one was adamant that the monkeys be removed so as to save the Monkey Baba and the holy atmosphere of his hermitage; the other was furious that these sacred animals were to be thus humiliated and turned from their rightful home. The battle lines had been drawn and everybody even remotely associated with the dispute felt compelled to involve themselves and make their voices heard. Sampath himself was forgotten in the fray, although his name was bounced back and forth between the warring factions like a ping-pong ball. Fairly spitting at each other, barely able to contain their wrath, their indignation and alarm, they fought from the minute they were allowed beneath Sampath's tree to the minute his visiting hours were over.

'How can you ask the monkeys to leave?' said Miss Jyotsna to everyone she met, supporting Sampath's point of view with loyalty.

'No one will be asking them, madamji. They will be kicking them out without asking them anything at all,' said one vulgar man.

But scores of people rushed to Miss Jyotsna's rescue. 'How can you say that? You have no shame.'

'Oh, rubbish,' said the spy, who was in an awful mood these days. 'Of course the monkeys should be done away with. They are cluttering up everything.'

People could not believe their ears. 'Did you hear what he said?' they asked each other. 'Rubbish, done away with, cluttering up . . .'

Miss Jyotsna turned around ferociously to face him. The two-faced hypocrite! Here he had been coming to the orchard every day, professing his affection for Monkey Baba, noting down everything he said, and now he was advocating something that could only bring Monkey Baba pain. In fact, if the monkeys were removed they would not even be able to call the Monkey Baba Monkey Baba any more, for there would be no more monkeys.

'Traitor,' she said, and, to everyone's surprise, especially Sampath's, pursing her small round mouth, gentle Miss Jyotsna swung at the spy with her handbag and hit him in the stomach so he was forced to leave immediately and catch a rickshaw home.

'Oh,' said Pinky and Ammaji admiringly. Perhaps this girl had something to her after all. This was quite a change from all that sentimental singing beneath the tree. But they were forced to side with Mr Chawla, who, to Miss Jyotsna's distress, said much the same thing as the spy, reasoning that the Baba might end up hurt and with rabies. At this, Miss Jyotsna did not know what to say and dissolved into tears. There seemed to be no solution to the problem.

Sampath was left worn out by these discussions, as if he himself had been caught hold of and pulled in various directions; as if he'd been stamped on and beaten black and blue. Yet, even though he was fatigued, every so often he was swept away on such a surge of anger, it was all he could do to keep from leaping up and throwing things, from yelling out loud or bursting into tears. Somewhere in the pit of his stomach a feeling of horrible anticipation had taken up permanent residence, and his head seemed possessed by an impenetrable fog. 'Hsssh,' he tried to calm himself. And: 'Hssh,' the breeze sounded about him. It seemed to Sampath that it shared his own concerns, that it was shushing him, soothing him. He tried to surrender himself to its gentleness, to its quiet, to the coolness that moved like a tender hand over his forehead, his cheek, his entire body.

The devotees made their way back down into Shahkot only to continue their arguments there, the sounds of their raised voices buzzing over the valley, rising from tea stalls, balconies and street corners.

In every neighbourhood, in every public venue, meetings and protest meetings were held. Meetings on the national level and the local level, in the religious interest and the civilian. A new Monkey Protection Society was formed with the support of the Cow Protection Society. A slew of members from the Atheist Society mingled unnoticed with the crowds. Every office, every family, seemed split over the matter. Business had come almost to a complete standstill as customers and shopkeepers refused to buy and sell from each other. 'See if I patronize your shop, you donkey!' 'What makes you think I'd sell to you, you son of a pig?' The police superintendent spent his days rushing about with his stick trying to break up the terrible fights that were taking place. There was no longer any peace in Shahkot.

19

In the meantime, in the midst of all this furore, Verma of the university had been working hard on his plan. After much thought and digging up of yellowing scientific documents, he finally drafted a proposal that involved a complicated procedure for the killing of the Cinema Monkey and a display of his carcass that would, Verma postulated, result in the disbanding of the entire troupe of monkeys. They would disband just like that and disappear quietly into the forest to join other faraway monkeys elsewhere. It was a beautiful plan and he delivered it personally to the house of the CMO, for ultimately he was in charge of all health matters in Shahkot. That, of course, included everything concerning carcasses and their display. Butcher shops, the burning ghats, laboratory work – all had to be met with his stamp of approval before anything else. Verma also sent photocopies of his plan to the District Collector still being awaited at his posting, to the Superintendent of Police and to other parties who would, he thought, be interested (for example, the *Indian Scientific Journal*, which had often published the articles of his colleagues).

He did not, however, show this plan to his wife, and though she was full of scorn for his ideas, seeing him retaliate in this way made her doubly angry. She began to plot and plan a separation from him. After all, they were not living in the dark ages, she thought. In their own town there was a man whose wife had left him, another who had left his wife and even someone who lived with a mistress, though nobody could understand why, for she was very plain.

The Brigadier too had come up with a plan. Sitting in his bathroom, waiting fruitlessly for the elusive green pigeon, the idea had hit him: he would organize an operation that would bring him honour and teach his men the true meaning of being in the army. It was his duty to take charge of all unusual and dire threats to peace and security. He would think of this mess as an opportunity rather than a bother.

'We could,' he suggested in a written report, 'organize a firing squad whereby fifty or a hundred men will be dispersed throughout the brush, discharging their rifles every twenty to forty minutes to scare the monkeys. If we persist, the monkeys will surely get the jitters and disappear from here, never to return.' And he sent army personnel in army jeeps to deliver his plan to the District Collector, who was expected by his secretary at the railway station very soon – if not on the next express from Delhi, then on the one after it. Also, copies were sent to the Superintendent of Police and the Chief Medical Officer.

The Chief Medical Officer did not receive this plan for he was sitting behind locked doors in a feverish state of advanced hypochondria. Drinking onion juice by the gallon, ignoring the persistent ring of the telephone, he was drafting, with a shaky hand, his own proposal for peace in Shahkot. You will be surprised, perhaps, to hear that a man so concerned with his own health could manage to drag his attention away long enough to think about the problem at hand, but he had his own interests at heart. If he was successful, he thought, with a leap of hope, surely he would be rewarded with a promotion. And promotion meant a transfer out of Shahkot. Oh, how he wished to be transferred out of this place of ill-health to one of peace and calm. Somewhere perhaps in the coastal regions of South India, for he had heard that in Kerala people were remarkably sophisticated and polite. And, no doubt, it would be restful to be near the ocean.

In elegantly worded prose that was one of his greatest strengths, he put forward his plan, which involved revoking the liquor licences of all shops and restaurants and banning alcohol in Shahkot. What a marvellous plan! He had thought of it while lying awake at night, unable to sleep, cushions piled up beneath him. What could be better for public health? And what better way to put a stop to the problem? With one fell stroke he would accomplish two such laudatory acts. Quite possibly this move would also put a damper on the problem of wife-beating, which had been getting rather out of hand of late. In that case, he could claim three . . . yes, three . . . victories! And he himself had nothing to lose as he was a strict teetotaller.

Carbon copies of his plan were delivered by government jeep to the railway station in preparation for the DC's still-anticipated arrival.

Only the Superintendent of Police, as you can see, had offered up no plan at all, for he didn't think of furthering his career. No. He did not want to be promoted for precisely the reason that the Chief Medical Officer *did*: it would mean a transfer out of Shahkot and he liked Shahkot. He liked the bazaar and the tea stall, he liked his naughty-eyed wife and all of his friends. It occurred to him that he might, in fact, be demoted because of all of this . . . Now that would not be such a bad thing . . . It would mean even more time to wander about the bazaar chatting with his cronies, even more time to sit with his wife eating golguppas in the municipal gardens while tickling her with flowers picked from the flowerbeds that had signs reading: 'Do not pick the flowers.'

Thus the Superintendent of Police did not join the others when they visited Sampath in order to seek his blessing for their plans. The CMO had been the first to decide to go. And as soon as the Brigadier heard of the proposed visit through a servant who had seen the officer driving to the orchard, he too leapt into his jeep. As he drove, he was spotted by Poncha and Sinha, Vermaji's friends, who persuaded a groaning Vermaji to join the procession on his moped. And so they all reached Sampath's tree within a half-hour of each other, each one of them accompanied by crowds of outraged citizens. There had been uproar, you see, when the plans just elaborated upon reached the ears of the population at large, leaked, as they were, by the drivers of the government and army jeeps and by Verma's wife, who had snooped among his papers in a way that should have made her ashamed.

Sampath had spent the morning looking at a collection of things he had made in an old tin can when he first arrived in the orchard. Still feeling a little uneasy in the head and stomach, he lay down like an invalid and tried to tempt himself with what had once been a great obsession. All sorts of things had gone into that tin: a red velvet-backed spider; a tall, thin seed case stacked with seeds like sheets of parchment; an orange bead of resin; a snakeskin; a bit of bone; feathers of various colours; soft silk cotton silk; the furry cape of a moth; a whorl of sepals; a leaf, diseased, freckled blue with fungus . . . Now, even though a lot of these things had grown faded or fallen to pieces, Sampath spread as much of his collection about him as he could, balancing the most precious items up and down his legs where they showed beautifully against his skin.

After about a month in the orchard, he had come to the conclusion that collecting was only worthwhile if you lived away from what you were collecting, not if you existed amidst all the bounty of your desire, not if you lived right where all you loved grew or crawled constantly by you. Anyway, how could you gather anything if you were wishing all the while that it would gather you up instead? Still, he felt nostalgic looking into his tin.

At this point he heard the noise of approaching protesters who accompanied the officials and Vermaji.

'Babaji,' shouted the CMO, the Brigadier and Vermaji, but it was impossible for any of them to speak, as there were so many disruptive people accompanying them. Bits and pieces of information at screaming pitch, garbled and incoherent, reached Sampath, whose bewildered mind would not have been able to make sense of it all even if they were straightforward in their speech. How he hated to be interrupted when he was intent upon something as interesting as the long-forgotten contents of his tin.

'Alcohol', 'Cinema Monkey', 'guns', 'banning', 'scaring', 'never to return', 'safety for your honourable self' . . . Spittle flew from mouths that were twisted into ugly expressions. The louder they were, the more hysterical they got. Sampath could see an unrecognizable look in their eyes. It came from no feeling he had ever seen in himself, and he had often run to the mirror so he could view how each of his emotions appeared upon his face. He did not think this method had worked entirely, for he was sure his face always altered in front of the mirror due to self-consciousness. But all the same, he was sure he could not have felt this emotion, which was stronger than the men who displayed it. What was it? It existed beyond a person and anything any person could be individually capable of. They shook with this gigantic force.

Sampath realized that he himself could speak out in a crowd only if he were happy; sadness or fright made him quiet. And anyway, he couldn't think of what to say . . . He couldn't think, and how could he respond when he didn't understand what they were saying? He couldn't understand, he couldn't . . . No . . . At one point he thought he heard one of his own lines being shouted back at him. Something about an elephant and a banana. 'Run when the elephant wants your banana.' Or: 'Eat a bun when the elephant wants your banana.' But no, surely not. These words were not like anything he would say. They sounded like gunfire, hit him like bullets. Like an accusation of guilt. But he was not guilty. No, no, he could not understand . . . All he knew was that this was nothing good for him, or for the monkeys, or the orchard, the birds and insects . . . or even the grass that was being so thoughtlessly trampled underfoot. Sampath rubbed a geranium petal against his lower lip, staining it red. He rolled a flower up and down his cheeks, colouring them to match his lip. He rattled a tamarind pod from his tin and ate a seed. He ate a bit of dried fern too, and in a nervous fit he swallowed the diseased leaf and began to chew on the bone. He felt fiery rage, yet he was also close to tears. Tremors ran through him. These people were trampling on him. They were invading him, claiming him, polluting the air about him. They were dirtying him with their dirty minds. How could they bring their horrible thoughts and ideas to him? And how dare they? They were using him for their own purposes. He felt sick.

Turning sour, his stomach revolted and fired up in a terrible state of indigestion as if it contained a roiling mass of serpents, venomous and hissing in volcanic heat.

Sampath leant over the edge of his cot and threw up. The vomit burnt him like acid, leaving his insides corroded and empty. Only the black hole of horrible anticipation he had felt for the past few weeks was left intact.

When the visitors were finally made to leave by Mr Chawla, they retreated not quiet and ashamed-looking, but shouting even louder to claim that the Baba's indigestion was the fault of whoever was arguing against them.

Sampath remembered his early rapture in the orchard. It had been a love affair: how he had bloomed and blossomed, how his joy, his playfulness had shone upon his face. He remembered, regarding the remains of his collection, how he had spent hours stringing necklaces of seed pods about himself. How he had put flowers behind his ears, sipped their nectar. He had unzipped pods with his teeth and prised open buds to uncover parasols of pink. The longer he spent in such activities, the more engrossed he had become. He had tickled his heel with the razor edge of wild grasses, rubbed his feet against a bit of bark to be overtaken by the same unbearable ecstasy that overtakes a cat rubbing itself against a tree trunk. He had squeezed the sticky gum from shrubs, cut into stems so the sap ran like milk and painted with the whiteness upon his legs. He had tapped anthers heavy with pollen so they spilled their rich yellow cargo on to his fingers and he had dusted this richness over his eyelids . . .

His mind returned to the afternoon's events.

20

It was into this strained atmosphere that the new District Collector was delivered when, at long last, the awaited express from Delhi arrived. As soon as he descended from the train, he found himself rushed at and surrounded by several stern-faced messengers and a secretary; they bore all sorts of plans and proposals on a subject about which, who knows how, he had not been briefed before his arrival.

'I am sorry, sir. I tried, sir,' said his secretary, 'but the phone lines are out and the postal and telegraph services are being run by my old boss, sir, who will not let me enter the premises, and we did not want to alert any of the big authorities for it would be better if we can deal with the situation ourselves . . . Or all the blame will be on our heads, sir, and it will go down as an immediate black mark on your record . . . Never mind, sir, in this way you will have had a nice peaceful journey instead of being worried . . . Am I right?' He beamed and garlanded the bewildered official with the garland of marigolds he had brought along, even though the flowers were rather bedraggled from having been at the station so long.

The newcomer was a quiet man and, though firm in his ideals, he was a very shy man, only just installed in government service, and very thin and weak-looking. He had been offered the town of Shahkot as his first posting precisely because it was not a very big responsibility, and so that he might find his feet gently, for, after all, his father was an influential officer in the Indian Administrative Service. How the family had rejoiced to have a new member in the government; after a short vacation to celebrate the news, he was sent on to his posting with thirty-five pickle jars containing pickles made personally by his mother, enough to last him two entire years in service! He had hoped to go home quietly with cook and driver, unpack, explore . . . and now . . . Black mark on records? What good is too much worry?

Who do you think this secretary was, giving all this fine advice in a waterfall of words? It was Mr Gupta from post-office days! Lonely after being more or less completely deserted by Miss Jyotsna and miserable in the post office with nobody to talk to but a curt and silent man hired in Sampath's place, he had applied for and obtained the post of secretary to the DC. At last, he felt, he was in the thick of things; more so, in fact, than at any other time in his life. His spirits rose. He would have been even happier if there had been a lady around to flirt with, of course, and he had been disappointed to learn the District Collector was a bachelor, but this job, he thought, might put him back in touch with Miss Jyotsna . . .

'I will escort you to your new home, sir. I myself gave orders for dinner. The cook is left over from the Raj, sir, and wanted to make you cutlets with caramel custard. I said: "Nothing doing. What did we get rid of the British for? To continue eating cutlets and custard?" You will have to be very strict with him. He got into a very bad mood, but I gave him orders for vegetable pulao and mutton curry. That is why he refused to come to the station. I am sure he is still sitting on his stool sulking . . . Oh, and after you have eaten, sir, we had better visit the Monkey Baba. It must be done, sir, or it will look bad. It is expected.'

In the meantime, swaying and jumping in the government jeep, the DC was trying hard to read the missives that had been delivered to him. He could not understand what was going on at all . . . and how his secretary could talk! He could not think, what with all the talking that man was doing. There, only a few days ago he had been on a blissful family vacation in Mussoorie and now here he was immersed in the worst governmental tragedy he could have dreamt of.

'These monkeys are a terrible business, sir,' said Mr Gupta, pretending hard to be unhappy, but looking, despite it all, very happy indeed.

21

The first meeting held with the Brigadier following the District Collector's arrival was stormed by the Monkey Protection Society. Terrified, the DC looked out of the window at the crowd of gargantuan proportions that seemed only to grow each time he turned his head to look again.

The evening before he had been taken to see Sampath in the guava orchard. Of course, he too had been accompanied by what Mr Gupta had referred to as 'rabble- rousers'. Shyly, for a moment, he had looked at Sampath and Sampath had looked at him. In a curious way, each of them had felt exposed and vulnerable to the other. Neither said a word as everybody else began, yet again, to have their say. Then Sampath had turned on his cot so he faced into the leaves and had refused to turn around again, so afraid was he of going through the same trauma that had caused him to be sick a few days ago. The DC felt a strong sympathy for the Baba and returned home even more distressed about the matter than before.

And now who knew what would happen at this meeting . . .

'Don't worry, sir,' whispered Mr Gupta, who had arrived for the meeting so early he was even in time to help the official heat his bath water with a makeshift immersion heater made of an electric coil about a wooden stick. 'I am here to give tip-top advice,' Mr Gupta whispered to him, smiling comfortingly. He liked his new boss much more than mean Mr D. P. S. from the post office.

The Brigadier seated himself across from the DC and Mr Gupta. He had been looking forward to presenting his clever plan to them. But no sooner had he opened his mouth than the crowd began to shout very loudly through the window. How was he supposed to talk with all these village bumpkins gathered around?

'What kind of military do we have in the country?' said angry voices. 'It is full of idiots. Firing guns every hour! We will not allow it. No guns in a holy place, no guns in a holy place, no guns in a holy place . . .'

'Do you even . . .' the Brigadier stuttered in response. 'Illiterate donkeys!'

'We will not stand for it,' interrupted a stern woman from the Monkey Protection Society and poked her thin head right into the room. 'No, we will not. We will absolutely, under no circumstances, stand for it.'

'Really, sir,' whispered Mr Gupta into the ear of the DC, 'it is a silly plan, sir. "Disperse men throughout the brush," he says here in his plan. But what brush, sir? Hundreds of people going up and down . . . it is more like a fairground than a brush. The bullets will be bound to hit somebody or other.'

'What, then, do you propose we do?' The Brigadier lost his temper at them all and leapt to his feet. 'Why don't you think of something yourselves? Why don't do you come up with an alternative plan, heh?'

'We should investigate peaceful options,' said a voice.

'Like what?' asked the Brigadier coldly and waited.

A silence fell upon the crowd.

'Negotiation,' said the Monkey Protection lady after a while.

'Oh hoh!' said the Brigadier with scorn and triumph. 'You try negotiating with a monkey, aunty.' And the seriousness of the protest was somewhat undermined as this picture of the stern Monkey Protection lady negotiating with the monkeys struck several people as being funny and they began, despite their fervent objection to his plan, to giggle rather inappropriately.

The DC looked at them amazed. How could they laugh? Just after they'd been shouting such angry threats . . .

Certainly, he reflected, he had come to a very unusual place. But this plan was inadmissible. His supervisor would be sure to hear of it and then, if there were any casualties . . . He must be firm about putting his foot down. 'If you don't mind my saying so,' he said to the Brigadier, 'this does not appear to be the most prudent of possibilities . . .'

Later in the morning they met with the CMO, who was accompanied by a crowd of angry businessmen and shopkeepers who had spent all night chanting slogans outside his bungalow. Gasping and pale, he dashed from the car to the DC's office under the guard of the police superintendent, who had been forced into duty yet again.

'We have received protests from all the shopkeepers, sir,' said Mr Gupta, giving the DC a quick briefing. 'They refuse to have their liquor licences revoked, and also we have received threats from all the surrounding towns saying if we revoke the licences, the monkeys will simply shift their focus and carry on being a nuisance in their vicinity. And they are right, sir, these monkeys might even teach their tricks to the local monkey populations in other towns if they are thrown out of this one. And then we will have a whole state of drunken monkeys. You yourself are familiar with the adage "One bad apple spoils the others." In this case we might say, "One bad monkey spoils the others."'

'But, sir,' shouted someone in the listening crowd, inspired by Mr Gupta's little witticism, 'can you really teach an old monkey new tricks?'

'Arreji,' said someone else, 'we will have enough problems with the young monkeys, whether the old ones are learning anything or not.'

'Yes, yes,' said Mr Gupta, 'this would be a case of "Stick your head out in wartime and be hit on the head."' He was enjoying showing off some of the lines he had learned from the Monkey Baba, especially since he had spotted Miss Jyotsna's admiring face in the midst of the crowd. In fact, he was amazed at how he could say these things and somehow, without him having to think, they meant exactly what he meant. He imagined being alone with Miss Jyotsna on a moonlit night. 'To make cream, you must churn the milk.'

Despite himself, the DC had begun to giggle. He felt surprisingly free. 'I do not know,' he said to the CMO, 'if this revoking of liquor licences would be the best idea . . .

The CMO was dismayed at how his plan was being greeted. 'Since this is the response I have been given,' he said in a dignified and injured tone, 'I might as well go home. I have another meeting to attend.'

'Is this the meeting with Vermaji, the scientist?' asked Mr Gupta with interest, and on hearing that it was, he turned to his boss. 'We had better join in, sir. He too has a proposal, if you recall, to get rid of the monkeys. If the CMO passes it, it will be presented to you.' He was loath to give up the fun and allow it to carry on somewhere else without him.

And so the three of them and their entourage of protesters travelled to the office of the Chief Medical Officer. On the way, the crowds gathered up their strength, even though they had been standing for quite a while now, and began to noisily shout their slogans. 'Dab your mouth with honey and you will get plenty of flies,' they shouted. 'Sweep before your own door. Your answers are beside the question. Many a pickle makes a mickle. Every bean has its black. Gather thistles and expect pickles? Show a clean set of teeth.'

'Do you hear them?' asked the DC, puzzled, his thoughts side-tracked. 'Many a pickle makes a mickle . . . what is a mickle? Guptaji, this town is full of adages I have never heard before.'

'When the buffaloes fight, the crops suffer,' the crowd continued. 'It is a hard winter when dogs eat dogs. Every cock fights best on his own dunghill. Puff not against the wind. Talk of chalk and hear about cheese!'

'Talk of chalk . . . and hear about cheese? Very odd. Where does this cheese come from?' The DC found himself most interested. He wished he could have stopped to ask them the meaning of all they were saying. 'Hear about cheese . . .'

While awaiting their arrival, Vermaji was sampling the tumbler of onion juice he had found sitting on the office desk in front of him, thinking, at first glance, that it was lemon squash. He took a gulp and immediately ran to the window to spit it out. He emptied the rest of the tumbler into the dry flowerbed.

'Terrible juice,' he said, making a face at the CMO when he entered. 'Why don't you drink orange instead?' he asked. 'Or pineapple?'

The temple people hammered on the door.

What a rude man, thought the officer, looking at the empty glass. First he had drunk all his onion juice and then, after that, he had had the audacity to criticize it. Why had he drunk it in the first place? Immediately he decided he was not going to approve Verma's plan. It was an absurd plan and why should he pass it when his own had been dismissed so readily? Nobody was considerate of him and he would not be considerate of Verma.

'Absolutely not,' he said.

'Why, what is wrong with pineapple juice? It's very nice juice,' said Verma, perplexed.

'I mean your plan,' shouted the CMO angrily. (Oh, and now he would get another stress-induced ulcer, he thought, in an immediate terrified aside.)

'But it is the one simple plan,' Verma pleaded, 'the one logical and scientific approach to what is after all a scientific problem of langur and human interaction, of alcohol addiction in monkeys – why can't it be approved?'

'It's a silly plan, that's why,' said Mr Gupta, although it was not his place to say anything. 'It will cause all sorts of bad smells and unsanitary conditions and that too in a holy place. And, no doubt, our fly problem would get worse.'

'We must categorically refuse your request,' said the CMO.

'Yes,' said the DC, who was still thinking of the adages.

But when at the end of the day they realized they had come up with no workable plan, they drove home somewhat subdued.

The police superintendent brought the DC the news that the monkeys had been on another expedition and raided the cupboards of the retired District Judge. They had taken five bottles of whisky and bounded away before the servants had even realized what had happened.

The DC went back to his bungalow and sat down worriedly. There he had been, laughing in a way he did only with his one close friend – miraculously his shyness had somewhat disappeared that day – but the problem had not been solved. He must not forget his responsibilities. He mulled things over, but could not think of anything that would raise his spirits. When the cook served his dinner, for it was already quite late in the evening, he was even further discouraged; he saw, with a sinking feeling of his heart, that his meal consisted of burnt-looking cutlets upon one of the grubbiest plates he had ever seen. Just where a pattern of flowers or, say, stripes should have been, the platter was stamped about with dirty fingerprints. The cook put it down before him with an unceremonious thump, then, without looking at the DC, turned and left.

Government officials did not know how to eat properly any more. The cook felt full of bitterness. And unable to make cutlets the first night, he had been struck with an unshakeable determination to make cutlets the second night. He made cutlets with a vengeance, a whole pile of them, and what insipid tasteless things they were – the DC was forced to bring out his mother's pickle to add a bit of flavour to his meal. He felt as miserable as ever.

Miserable as ever, and alone, sitting there by himself at one end of the huge dining table. A bare bulb dangled from a wire above him and cast a dim light upon the table, while the rest of the room disappeared into darkness around him. The windows were black, gaping holes to his right and left. Sad, dirty curtains hung limply at their sides. He got up, drew the grey fabric together and sat back down to his cutlets. Oh, how would he be able to finish the awful, charred things?

Just as he was wondering whether to flush them down the toilet, he was interrupted by Mr Chawla.

'Who is it?' said the DC, alarmed.

'It's the Monkey Baba's father,' said Mr Chawla and,

opening the flimsy wooden door that led in from the front veranda, he stepped inside. 'I too,' he said firmly, 'have a proposal to make.'

'What proposal?' asked the DC, putting down his knife. A wave of tiredness swept over him. It had been a long day. He took off his spectacles and rubbed his eyes.

'Let us train the army and police as monkey catchers,' said Mr Chawla. 'Decide on a day in the near future and catch all the monkeys in one go. We can use the army trucks to convey them to a far-off forest, preferably in another state, from where it will be impossible for them to return or to obtain any liquor. They will have to resume the life they should be leading as monkeys, eating forest fruits and nuts.'

The DC sat back, considering what he had heard. There seemed to be no problem with that . . . Who on earth could object? Monkeys eating forest fruits and nuts . . . It painted a very pretty picture. Provided it would work. At first glance, anyway, it was a harmless enough proposal. And this was the Baba's father who was proposing this plan. Surely he would do only what was best for his son. With a rush of compassion, he remembered Sampath, who had turned his back on him when he paid a visit to the orchard. 'Perhaps you have thought of something,' he said, playing with his cutlets. And he thought it over some more.

Mr Chawla stood and waited.

He had not been moved to laughter or shouted slogans like the other fools during the day's earlier meetings. The orchard had disintegrated into a sorry state and he knew his life there was in danger of drawing to a close. Already, the flow of money into the bank accounts was dwindling. There were no more talks, no more gentle evenings; there was no more laughter. Sampath sat miserably, as if hiding now, in his tree. And Mr Chawla had noticed the way his son was slipping back into his old silences, into his old opaque and unhappy manner, the way his eyes were losing their quiet, contented look and glazing over. His good humour and his sense of fun had disappeared altogether, and ever since the DC's visit he had stayed facing the leaves, preoccupied, for all his father knew, with the thought of leaving. What if Sampath should climb down from the tree, run away and spoil everything? No, this would not do. Things would have to be resolved. The monkeys would have to be dealt with and peace restored. And clearly, he thought, after the day's meetings and discussions, you could not leave anything to bureaucratic ineptitude. He had grown steadily more frustrated through all of the day's earlier plans and meetings. Behind this frustration, though, there was something more: a terrible sadness and a feeling of vulnerability he did not wish to investigate, though it lapped against his immediate concerns, giving him, despite himself, the unsettling feeling of being afloat upon an infinite ocean. He would not, could not, consider this. To think of such things, he was sure, would mean drilling holes in his watertight heart; all sorts of doubts would pour in and he would be a lost man.

'What do you think of my plan?' he asked the DC.

The District Collector moved a bit of cutlet from one end of the plate to the other. 'Yes,' he said again, more certainly this time, 'perhaps you have thought of something.' The proposal involved no guns, no religious matters, no business interests that he could see. It should at least be given a try. And he was the DC, after all, he remembered with a rush. If he said 'Yes', it meant 'Yes.' As firmly as he could, he said: 'Yes, this is a workable plan. Of course, the Baba will have to descend from his tree temporarily, or he might suffer injury,' and he ate the last bit of pickle on his plate and pushed away his cutlets. 'Khansama,' he shouted to the cook, 'please do not make cutlets ever again. Never ever. No cutlets, no fish fry, no mutton chops, no aloo mash, no vegetable boil, no tomato soup, no fritters, no trifle, no caramel custard, no English food . . .' He practically panted as he said this.

The cook appeared at the doorway, stood for a minute in his soiled red coat with a filthy black dishrag over his shoulder and then gave the DC a look of withering scorn. Without a word, he turned and disappeared back down the black corridor into the reaches of the cavernous and sooty kitchen.

On Monday evening the monkeys returned from the English Wine and Beer shop tipsy. On Wednesday they attempted to break into the Club for Retired Members of the Court. And on Thursday they held to ransom top-secret documents in the army's headquarters that outlined safety precautions taken by the Indian army against invasion. They would not give them up until they were bribed with bottles from the bar in the mess.

With remarkable speed, the necessary permission for Mr Chawla's plan was granted, the requisite papers stamped, orders given to the army and police, and a date set for Monday, the last day of April, for Sampath's temporary descent from the tree and the capture and transport of the Shahkot monkeys to a destination far away from Shahkot.

'I will not descend,' said Sampath.

'But the descent is temporary. You can climb down and then, a few hours later, you can climb back up.'

But Sampath did not quite believe this. If he climbed down, somehow, he was sure, he would not get to climb up again. No doubt they would try to bundle him into some outrageous hermitage. Anyway: 'I will not live without the monkeys,' he said firmly, holding on to his initial position and not in the mood for compromise. Beneath his tree Miss Jyotsna wept.

Ammaji gave her a dirty look. 'Why don't you go home for a while?' she said, nudging her with a fly swatter. 'You are spoiling his mood even more.'

Kulfi winked kindly at her son, but her thoughts were far away. A monkey, she thought, and her eyes gleamed, looking like dark lakes pierced by sun. A monkey. How would she cook this fascinating monkey? On the last day of the month of April . . .

Should she bake it in a tandoor? Simmer and stew it? Stuff or fry it? Roll it into banana leaves, fill it into chickens or goose eggs? Mix it into a naan? Seal it in an earthen pot? Season it with saffron? Scent it with cloves? Cook it with pomegranate juice?

Sampath looked and found no help in the faces of his family. How much had changed since he had first arrived in the orchard such a short time back. How quickly it was becoming more and more like all he hoped he had left behind for ever. Ugly advertisements defaced the neighbouring trees; a smelly garbage heap spilled down the hillside behind the tea stall and grew larger every week. The buzz of angry voices and the claustrophobia he had associated with life in the middle of town were creeping up upon him again. And now they were getting rid of his favourite company in the orchard! Didn't they know how fond he was of the monkeys? And didn't they know how little he cared for all of *them*? Why didn't they take their advertising, their noise and dirt, their cars and buses and trucks, why didn't they take their little minds and leave him to his peace and quiet, to his beloved monkeys, to his beautiful landscape that was being so dirtily and shoddily defaced?

He would have to escape. But how? How could anyone manage this? They would not let him go. If he descended from the tree, they would catch him. If he stayed, things would only get worse. He recognized the old feeling of being caught in a trap . . .

Oh, but he would have to leave! How, how, how? He thought, but his thoughts found no resolution and merely revolved, more and more of the same, around and around in his head. At last, from what the devotees could observe, he fell into a sort of stupor.

'Let him be,' said his father. 'On the morning of 30 April we will bring him down and, before he knows it, it will all be over.'

'All be over . . .' Sampath heard, as if from very far away.

22

A few days after Mr Chawla had proposed his plan, it was put into action. The monkey catchers began to be trained at a furious pace, even though nobody was quite sure what exactly the training should consist of. The Brigadier, who was still holding a grudge because his own idea had been passed over in favour of this weak and messy plan, shouted orders at his suffering men through his megaphone, putting them through their paces, making them leap from trees, slide down ropes, do handstands and sit-ups, and go running for miles up and down the hillside, so much so that people complained that not only were the monkeys disturbing the peace but those wretched army boys were as well. Thudding across gardens and trampling flowers, they ran through private property and left trails through flowerbeds and vegetable fields, waking people at dawn the next day, and every day after that, by resuming these disgraceful activities. The very ground trembled as they approached; it was like the approach of an earthquake.

But when the Brigadier received complaints, he explained how, had he been allowed to pursue his own proposal, he would have no reason to submit his men to this charade. They all knew how to fire guns. They would have gone to the orchard and, a couple of hours later, the job would have been done. Now, since they had not supported him right at the beginning, they would have no option but to suffer. 'Sit up, double march, hop to it, somersault,' he ordered. And: 'The sooner this is all over the better,' mumbled the townsfolk.

Meanwhile, the police were luckier than the army men, for it had been generally agreed upon that they were incapable of taking an active part in something on such a great scale as this and instead they had been given the job of preparing the nets that were to be used to catch the monkeys. Under the gentle jurisdiction of the superintendent, they sat lazily outside the police station with a pile of fishing nets and metal rings, needles and nylon rope, not at all sure of what they ought to be doing, but enjoying themselves like old fisherwomen fussing with the nets in the afternoon sun. 'Arre, Chottu,' they called to the tea boy. 'Arre, over here,' to the sweet-potato seller, the peanut man and the cold-drink cart. Thus they made the most of this time and were content.

About Sampath's tree there was a feeling of the air being stretched tight and wrapped around and around him. When he peered down, all he could see was an ugly sea of humanity. Nobody respected his visiting hours any more. Several men marched about the periphery of the orchard, banging the ground with sticks and blowing upon whistles in a round-the-clock watch instituted by Mr Chawla to give warning of any disturbance. These dangerous days, who knew what would happen, what they would have to watch out for, which unexpected happening? They were not safe. Also, of course, they had to keep a watch for the monkeys. What would they do next? At the slightest rustle in the night, they shone bright torches into the trees; often Sampath found himself awakened by a searchlight-like glare. If only these watchmen would fall asleep at their posts the way watchmen were known to do, thought Sampath. But no, this lot were an insomniac brigade, tireless and unnervingly zealous in their duties. At the first hint of dawn, the crowds arrived with their loudspeakers and he was enveloped once again in slogan-shouting and argument.

How, how would he manage his escape?

He was practically ill with worry and nerves by now, unable any more to sleep and unable to eat. His mother tried this and that to tempt his appetite, to resurrect his fading rosy cheeks, but nothing seemed to work . . . not the little river fish he so loved, not the fiery chillies from her own especially fiery chilli bush, not the plump, sleepy pigeons with their tender melting flesh, not an enormous goldfish she caught in the ornamental pond in the convent grounds. Never mind . . . never mind. Soon she would offer him something altogether new, something to spark his spirits and jerk him to life. On Monday, the thirtieth day of April. She began to put together the ingredients for the feast to come. It was a hard process, for the main ingredient was an entirely new one, of course, and still mysterious to her. She had no idea of its savour, its toughness, its heaviness or lightness, its darkness, or its power as a catalyst to bring other flavours to fullness. Her preparations would have to be made with only instinct to guide her, the sureness of instinct, buoyed by a bringing together of all her expertise, all her talents, to make a triumph of what might be her only chance to cook this creature . . .

Sampath stared up into the mountains, tilting his head all the way back, to look upon where there was not a trace of civilization. There, up high, as if tumbling from the sky, a waterfall cascaded down sylvan slopes, so pale, so distant he did not know if it was real or merely his imagination melding with the power of sight to produce a trick upon him. There there were no villages, no houses, no people . . .

Just sunlit forest and rock, and the living rough white water. Jealously, he looked back at the birds that fluttered about him searching for crumbs: these small creatures with their delicate ribs, their beating wings that scooped hearts light as snow through the clarity of air. His face bore a desperate, hunted look.

'He is in another world,' whispered the devotees reverently, while Sampath paid them no attention, just stared out over their heads, let them lift his foot and lay it upon their heads as they claimed his blessing. These days it turned his stomach, now that the whole business was not lighthearted any more, but mean and complicated.

He stared at the sky. The silvery evening air seemed to distil itself into the armour of the fish that steamed gently before him, into the powdery hair of the langurs sitting in his tree, still unaware, it seemed, of all the plotting and planning that was going on against them. There they were, chattering, playing, grooming each other as usual. Little did they know . . .

23

Trapped in his room, aunties and sisters keeping watch out of every window, the Hungry Hop boy paced up and down. From a distance, he could hear the noise of the protesters and demonstrators, and he felt it was unjust that he should not be allowed out to take part in the excitement.

'I'll take the van,' he pleaded. 'It will be such good business.'

But no, even this was not enough to shake his family's conviction that he should be kept firmly locked up, allowed to emerge only if rooted in the honourable state of wedlock. In the matter of a few days' time, the Hungry Hop boy had been demoted from a life of self-imposed imprisonment to one of family-enforced detainment and he felt as if his pride were being overlooked and insulted. He paced up and down his small room, wondering about Pinky's fate in the midst of all the monkey trouble, about his own fate . . . Up and down. And whenever he stopped to listen, with an indignant ear pressed against the door, he could hear the babble of marriage negotiations rising up the stairs from the living room down below. Time was running out. They were resorting to the oldest trick in the book.

He smuggled an urgent note to Pinky via the faithful milkman, who delivered it when he returned home on the same bus Sampath had taken when he had first left Shahkot six months ago. 'Very little time to lose,' the note read, a little runny from a leftover bit of buffalo milk in the canister where the milkman had placed it. 'Marriage is in the works.'

As he waited for a reply, he paced the length of his room with greater and greater vigour. From time to time, he stopped and tossed back his hair, a thrill running through him like an electric current. Here was his life, just like in a scene from the movies. He felt grateful for the glamour; his heart hung suspended as if dangling from a mountain ledge.

By the next morning he had a response from Pinky who did not believe in delays. In a firm hand, she proposed they escape in the Hungry Hop van and drive far away, to a new town, a new place where they would not have to bother with his unreasonable family. That seemed the only available option. 'On Monday, 30 April,' read her practical note, 'they are going to catch the monkeys. Everybody will be busy and paying no attention. Meet me under the big tamarind tree on the street leading to the orchard-bazaar road at 5.00 a.m. in the Kwality van, and from then on we will see.'

Monday, 30 April . . . that was only three days away! Seized by courage, Hungry Hop wrote back with a trembling hand: 'Without fail I will be there.'

Although, once she received this note, Pinky was caught up in her own absorbing affairs of packing her belongings and getting ready to leave – all in secret, of course – she could not help feeling sorry for her brother. It did not seem quite fair, she thought, that just when her life was blossoming and flourishing, his should be cut down and curtailed. This she felt, even though her own feelings towards the monkeys were so different from his. Generous in these days of love, she climbed up the ladder against his tree. 'I have an idea,' she said.

But Sampath, back to his old ways of barely speaking, merely looked blankly at her and said nothing at all in response.

'You know,' she continued, 'perhaps you can come along with the Hungry Hop boy and myself, for, you know,' she whispered loudly, 'we are planning to elope, you know.'

Who knows why she had to put in so many 'you know's?

'I am not going to climb down from this tree,' said Sampath.

'But why not?' said Pinky, climbing back down the ladder hastily when she saw the Cinema Monkey approaching to sit in his accustomed place by Sampath on the cot. 'We can go all over in the van and travel from one place to another.'

Sampath thought of endless roads in the endless sticky summer that would arrive so very soon to stretch before them, of trucks billowing out exhaust, the vibration of engines through his head, nausea rising from his stomach, and he felt unbearably hot and then cold as ice. He thought of his old life in the post office, of the people milling about him, pushing him, shoving him in the streets, and he felt as ill as when the officials had visited him. In fact, he almost lost his balance and fell from the tree. In the background a loudspeaker crackled and the words ran into a nonsensical blur. His face had gone white.

'What's the matter with you?' asked Pinky, alarmed.

'Thank you for asking,' he managed to say. 'But it is better that you go on your own.'

'Why is it better?' Pinky demanded, exasperated.

'Because it is,' he shouted loudly and angrily, suddenly irritated by all of it and everybody. They would kill him. He would just die. 'Leave me alone, I am going to be sick. Leave me alone, leave me alone, leave me alone . . .'

'Oh, well,' said Pinky, going away. He was very whiny today, wasn't he? Who would have thought he would ever have had the enterprise to run away from home and into a tree? For a little while her brother had shown some character and now he was going backwards, as usual . . .

Little did she know of the events going on in the Hungry Hop household at that very moment, or she would not have been wasting her time talking to him in this fashion.

The day before Hungry Hop was to elope with Pinky, he was introduced to the girl his relatives had picked to be his future wife.

Though it is usually customary for the boy's family to visit the girl's, due to the unusual circumstances regarding Hungry Hop, his family arranged for things to be done the other way around instead. Before this chosen girl arrived, sandwiched fondly and closely between her parents in a rickshaw, Hungry Hop surpassed himself by throwing the biggest tantrum he had ever subjected his family to. They grew nervous at his fits of temper, the slamming of doors, his locking himself up, his emerging to shout something down the stairs, his locking himself up again . . .

'But she is a very sweet girl,' they pleaded. 'Just take a quick look. She is pretty and good-tempered and you will like her.' Really, his character had changed since he had been bitten by Pinky. Never did he used to lose his calm . . . They shook their heads over it all yet again.

'If you like her so much,' he said rudely, 'marry her yourself and let her give you bother and trouble.'

'But, son, just . . .'

'You are eating my head,' he interrupted, slamming another door.

But in the end, curiosity got the better of him and he went downstairs quietly enough when the girl arrived. He would look at her and then, with even a greater number of arguments to boost his point of view, he could, in all fairness, refuse her. He wore a white shirt and white trousers and, still a little thundery-looking about the eyes, he entered the room.

And . . .

Oh, but oh, who can plan against the powers of fate?

What a girl! What a girl he saw sitting demurely between an ugly Mummy–Papa when he stepped around the curtain hanging in the doorway of the room! She surpassed anything he could have ever expected. So plump, so pink and white! A complexion like that under the Indian sun! With such a sleepy face and sleepy eyes, such a good-natured sleepy smile . . . He could not believe his eyes! Her sari was rosebud-coloured, her cheeks were like vanilla pudding, her mouth like the rose on top of the icing of a birthday cake . . . Yes, he thought, she was exactly like a birthday cake, a pink and white birthday cake . . . The pearls in her ears and about her neck and wrists were like the little silver decoration balls. He opened his mouth and stared.

All about the room, his sisters and aunties, his grandmother and mother nudged each other. This girl had failed every examination she had ever taken, it was true, but there was something to her, wasn't there? They were very pleased and proud with the good job they had done despite the difficult circumstances.

Hungry Hop retreated, his head in a whirl. When she left, his family closed in upon him, filling his ears with talk, bribing him with promises of a Maruti car and television, a wedding party of two weeks in duration . . . Stop! he thought to himself. How can I do this? But they continued and a pleased look could not help but show through the grumpy one he tried hard to maintain.

When they left, all his doubts filed back into his brain and that night, when he was supposed to meet Pinky the next morning, he did not sleep a wink. He tossed and turned until his sheet wound uncomfortably and tightly about his legs. His thoughts tumbled and jumped, interrupted each other and became entangled in themselves. On one hand, he had given his word he would meet Pinky the next morning and he was a nice boy, after all . . . On the other hand, just think of how easy and pleasant it would be if he stayed . . . But yet, he felt embarrassed to give in so easily after he had made such a fuss before his family and held out for so many days. He thought of Pinky and all her notes and presents, her biting his ear and hitting him on the jaw. It was true, Pinky had something to her too. Nobody could deny that. And just that morning, it had seemed so exciting – he would jump into the van and drive away. But now . . . he didn't know . . . he didn't know . . . There was the girl like ice cream, like birthday cake, like wedding cake . . . Oh, look, now he was saying wedding cake, not birthday cake, and that seemed heavy with peculiar significance . . . even though they would not have wedding cake at his wedding, of course, but laddoos.

At 4.00 a.m. he rose, his mind still not made up, and sneaked out to the van. Amazingly, as if by fate, nobody heard him – they were sleeping soundly, sure of work well done and a safe future for their son. They slept and snored as if resting after months of unease and worry. Quietly he pushed his van down the road and only when he turned the corner did he start the engine and get in. He would drive to the tamarind tree and there, depending on how he felt, he would tell Pinky that this was impossible, or he would sweep her up and drive away in the Hungry Hop van . . . He took a maze of little side streets instead of the one-way main road so he might have plenty of opportunities to turn quickly around and return home, if that was the decision he made, or to move to the main road, if that was what he wanted. 'Pinky or Miss Pudding and Cake,' he muttered to himself. 'Pinky or Miss Pudding and Cake . . .'

Deliriously, he drove in circles through the shadowed streets, when, all of a sudden, he became aware of a huge grey group of people and cars coming up fast behind him and remembered with a start that this was the day they were to catch the monkeys. No doubt these were the monkey catchers themselves, on their way to the orchard just like him!

'Get out of the way,' they shouted at him. 'Get out of the way.'

Urgently he tried to turn into another street, but it was very narrow and his van got stuck. Such things are wont to happen at crucial moments in one's life, of course, and it took him quite a while to turn into yet another side lane, to embark upon yet another loop of his journey. 'Pinky or Miss Pudding and Cake . . .' Or nobody, for that matter! Nobody! They were making his life a misery.

24

By 4.00 a.m. in the District Collector's bungalow, the DC
was awake and dressed so as to be ready when Mr Gupta
arrived, which he did soon after, bundled in a copious
number of woollen scarves and a cheerful yellow hat,
knocking excitedly in staccato fashion on the door.
Together, they were to go in the government jeep to the
cantonment area. Here they would join the army, who
would be armed with the nets, and together they would
proceed to the orchard, where they would meet the police,
who were to be on special alert for any disturbance that
might interrupt these sensitive operations. Sampath would
be brought down from the tree into police custody, the nets
would be unloaded, the soldiers would get into the battle
formation drawn up by the Brigadier and capture the monkeys. By the time the sun was properly in the sky, it would
all be over.

But when, at 4.05 a.m., according to schedule, the DC
and Mr Gupta were seated in the government jeep going
down the driveway that led from the bungalow to the road,
they had not proceeded more than a few yards when suddenly the driver braked. There, blocking the driveway,
spread out all over, was a huge and motley collection of
bundles and bed rolls, of broken chairs and tables, battered
pots and pans galore, some dirty quilts and old pillows
with stuffing coming out of them . . . Even an ancient rusty-

spring bed and two skinny goats were visible in the predawn light! What was more, they could hear a dreadful banging and clanging, and a loud scraping coming from the servants' quarters that stood just to the side of the driveway.

'What on earth is going on there?' said the DC as Mr Gupta leapt from the jeep to find out. The air was filled with the musty smell of mouldering objects that had clearly not been out in the open air for years.

Mr Gupta returned a minute later. 'It is the cook – he is leaving for his ancestral home. He says he is not going to stay here to be insulted in his old age. I think, sir, it is all unfortunately about the cutlets. I told him: "Kindly move your belongings from the driveway immediately." But he says he is too old to do anything quickly and as it is he does not care at all.'

'Oh dear, we will be late,' said the DC, and they were forced to descend from the jeep and move for themselves, all the odds and ends the cook had collected over sixty-five years in government service. Who knows how the old man had managed to drag it all out in the first place? As they worked, the cook continued the racket he was making from inside his lodgings.

It was quite some time before they had nudged the stubborn goats into the bushes and succeeded in clearing all the cook's belongings from the path. In fact, a whole half-hour was wasted before the driver, the DC and Mr Gupta were able to continue upon their way.

At precisely this time in the army cantonment area, the lights were blazing from the barracks and men, already dressed in khaki uniforms, were gathering about the flag pole. At the appointed time the Brigadier appeared as well and, marching to the main gates, spick and span, he got into his personal jeep.

'Ready?' he barked. 'Well, then, onward mar –'

It was at this point, even though the sky was only just beginning to lighten, that he spotted, with his eagle eyes, his heart's desire: there, in the old mulberry tree by the gate, the modest green pigeon who had so long teased, maddened and seduced him with its liquid notes, its reminders, sweet . . . piercing . . . of the old film songs that his mother had listened to when he was a child. Ah, that haunting sadness, that limpid voice pouring heart-rendingly from the throat of Lata Mangeshkar, a voice that sang of death and lost love, of lotus-flower feet and sandalwood skin, of long dark eyes, of loneliness, and the ache, the dreadful ache, of memory. All this and more he remembered from the few notes that sounded in the trees by his house. All this and more, he thought, from this small, drab bird sitting silent now upon the branch.

'A net!' he hissed. 'Quick, a net, a net . . .' Urgently, he prodded a surprised soldier with his baton. Then, snatching a monkey net from the startled man, he jumped from the jeep and threw it at the green pigeon in a blind desire to capture this elusive bird, to keep it by him as he lived in the army cantonment, to torture himself with the memory of his childhood, of his mother, whom he had loved so fiercely . . .

The net was far too big and too heavy, of course, for a single man to toss after a bird, and it travelled only a few feet before falling to the ground with a heavy thump, a pile of cumbersome nylon rope. With a slight flutter past his ears, the green pigeon rose and, before his horrified eyes, flew away, high over his head, to who knows where.

'Damn!' The Brigadier smashed his fist down upon his palm. 'Damn, damn, damn.' It was a bad omen. But then, who was he to believe in omens? 'Forward march, you damn fools,' he said angrily to his men when he became aware of the stares turned in his direction. And they hurried off, having forgotten meanwhile to wait for the DC and Mr Gupta, who finally alerted their attention by blowing their horn loudly as they approached, driving full speed about the bends in the road, catching hold of whatever part of the jeep they could as they rattled and leapt over the rubble. When they caught up and the procession was complete, they started again. Now, hopefully, there would be no more delays. 'Come on now. Move quickly, we are late . . . Double march . . . Left, right . . . Left, right . . . One, two . . . One, two . . . Left, right. Left –'

And they double-marched, it is sad to report, left right left, straight into another pile of suitcases and bedding rolls spread mysteriously upon the road.

'Oh, no,' roared the Brigadier. 'What now?'

'Who would have thought there'd be so many problems at this hour?' said Mr Gupta, lowering a scarf he had wrapped about his mouth to keep the chill out. 'We especially chose this time for lack of traffic and obstructions, and now just see what is happening.'

There, swaddled in even more woollens than Mr Gupta, in the midst of a sea of suitcases, was the CMO, giving orders to a small army of servants in front of his bungalow. Several cars spilled from his driveway on to the road.

'What are you doing, fatso?' shouted the Brigadier.

The CMO turned pale. 'Are you referring to me?' he asked with dignity. 'If so, I think you should keep your words to yourself until you know the state of my health!'

'Move,' shouted the Brigadier. 'Move, move, move yourself and your bloody belongings. Now!'

'But where are you going?' asked Mr Gupta.

'Don't start up a conversation . . . We are late, can't you see?' The Brigadier turned on him.

'Due to health problems, I have been forced to take vacation leave in Kasauli. Every now and then, you know, in times of stress –'

'Just move,' shouted the Brigadier in purple rage. 'Move your hundreds of damn suitcases.'

'Oh dear,' said the DC, watching the ensuing hullabaloo, 'and I myself signed that vacation leave. I suppose it was my fault.' He was feeling very nervous and miserable again. Clearly all the decisions he had made had been bad ones. First the cook and the insult to his cutlets and then the CMO and his vacation. Now the problem with the monkeys would just get worse, a scandal would erupt, his father would hear of it and feel embarrassed . . . Oh, it was a terrible business. If only he had gone into computers, that would have been a nice quiet life . . .

In a while they began to move again. But: 'Do not go that way, sir,' advised an alert sweeper man from the CMO's house. 'You will be stopped again in front of Vermaji's house as soon as you turn the corner. His wife is moving out. It is a very shameful matter.'

Dark as a monsoon cloud, the Brigadier spat out orders for the cavalcade to back out of the road they had come on and to take another and, for that matter, much longer route out of town. By the time they finally reached the orchard, no doubt the monkeys would have disappeared and they would have to repeat this ridiculous charade another day.

They turned the corner on to the new road and, no sooner had they proceeded a short way down its pot-hole-ridden length than, there in front of them, they spotted the dumpy shape and brightly painted sides of the Hungry Hop van.

'Pinky or Miss Pudding and Cake . . .'
A black stream of dirty exhaust billowed and puffed into
the army men's faces.

25

In the orchard, meanwhile, things were remarkably quiet. In a corner, something in a big pot steamed and simmered with a gentle bubbling sound. It had been bubbling all night already, in preparation for the monkey catchers' arrival. Kulfi slept near it. As the men absorbed themselves in catching the monkeys, she had thought she would somehow, by hook or by crook, direct the fall of one of the animals right into the cooking pot. Then she would drown it immediately away from attention into a delicious gravy. This was the plan. How exactly it would work, she was not quite certain, but she knew that in the midst of the ensuing confusion she would manage it. The scent of herbs and fruit, of spices and seasonings, filled the air and consequently everyone who slept on the hillside that night dreamt of food, from the watchman's shed at the top of the road, all the way down into the valley where the police superintendent was still wrapped cosily in his blanket. They dreamt of magnificent banquets, of ladles and spoons so big that battalions of cooks had to be employed in carrying them through vast fogs of steam to simmering cauldrons that spluttered and glowed . . .

'A bushel, a drachm, a pint,' muttered Kulfi in her sleep. 'A peck, a coomb, a sack, a hogshead, a scruple, a ton. Sandal, madder, cassia, orris root.' She turned restlessly. 'Gall nut, cinnabar, mace. Senna, asafoetida, quail eggs, snail eggs, liver of a wild boar, tail of a wild cat . . .' She turned around again. 'Nasturtium leaves, rhododendron flowers, cicada orchids!' She sat bolt upright. The delicate white and wood-green flowers of the cicada orchid. What would her dish be without them? A tasteless dish, not even half what it should be, a failure, a disappointment. An utter disaster.

She would have to go and fetch this flower, wouldn't she? She must have it, this exquisitely flavoured, graceful, transparent flower that hinted of moss and forest. She must have it and she must have it immediately! She looked around to see how the night was thinning . . . It was almost dawn. There was just enough time for her to go up the hillside and back before the monkey catchers arrived. Hurriedly dressing, she took up her spade, her sickle and a coil of rope and disappeared into the shadows, passing as she did so, the spy, who was already hiding in the bushes awaiting the morning's drama.

Running a high temperature because of the excitement and nervousness he was experiencing, he awaited the dawning of this day that would, he was determined, in the midst of chaos, deliver to him the opportunity he had been waiting for so long: the opportunity to discover exactly what stewed in those cauldrons of Kulfi. 'If you have a monkey, you will not get lice. To make curd, don't unsettle the milk. Does a pond clean the mud at its bottom? Does the rain wash the sky? As is the wood, is the meat cooked upon it.' The past few months had turned him into a man tormented. The lines in his head were like jungle vines entangling him, smothering him. He would have to break free, prove his character to the world. And to himself.

As Kulfi passed by on her way to the forest, she walked so near to where he was squatting, the edge of her sickle knife tickled his nose, but she went on without noticing him.

She did not stop to check on Sampath either, or the rest of the family, which was all for the best, since otherwise she might have noticed the absence of Pinky, who was already waiting under the tamarind tree for Hungry Hop, dressed and ready, just as planned, although she was in an extremely bad temper for some reason she was not able to determine. Yes, who knows why, but she was feeling exceptionally irritable, dissatisfied and angry. Maybe it was just a lack of sleep. As she waited, she hit against the side of the road with a stick. If only Sampath had come along, she would have had somebody to talk to . . .

But Sampath sat in the guava tree, encased in absolute stillness like a fossil captured within a quiet moment of amber. The watchmen had been dismissed for once, so the monkeys might not be disturbed on this, their last night in the orchard; that they might be in the tree, barely awake, when the monkey catchers arrived.

Sampath had been sitting still a long while. He had watched as the last of the sun disappeared the evening before, as the hills turned soft and blue like woodsmoke and as the bushes, gathering shadow since late afternoon, merged with the darkening air. He had felt the breeze against his cheek, heard the sound of the crickets start up, the first frog's awkward inquiry into the evening, its rising, ginger croak growing stronger with the night that leaked from the soil and ran from the dark shapes about him. It had seeped from the black bellies of the underground tubers, from the hidden pods of seeds and flowers, from the inky beetles and the hollow-hearted bamboo. He saw the white petals of the night flowers unfold, a speckling of bright stars appear above him; smelled the jasmine his mother had planted and the poisonous datura, watched the wan moths ford the blackness to hover lovelorn over a tobacco flower. Lifting his finger, he traced the magical shapes of constellations, creating them at whim, then let his hand drop back into his lap again.

The night wore on. Down below, all was silent. Still Sampath sat and watched. Once he felt a flutter of terror about his heart, but he did not follow it to its source, did not think ahead to what was to happen the next day, and the flutter died down as quickly as it had started. Hour upon hour went by. The hour of midnight passed. It was Monday, the last day of April, and all was quiet in the orchard. The family slept and the monkeys were silent in the guava tree.

There were ways of thinking about darkness. He could steel himself against it, Sampath thought, close his eyes tight, wrap himself up in his quilt. Or he could let all its whisperings, all its shades of violet, float into him. This impersonal darkness could be comforting as no human attention ever was. He felt the muscle in him relax, and as time drew on he felt strangely calm, felt his thoughts drop away and a strange strength enter into him, a numbness seeping into his limbs. From exhaustion, or resignation, or faith in some new inspiration, who knows? He could not feel the trunk of his body any more, but his senses were not numbed. They grew sharper and he was acutely aware of every tiny sound, every scent and rustle in the night: the stirrings of a mouse in the grass, the wings of a faraway bat, the beckoning scent that drew the insects to hover and buzz somewhere beyond the orchard. Underground, he could hear water gurgling, could hear it being drawn into the trees about him; he heard the breathing of the leaves and the movements of the sleeping monkeys.

Here and there in the branches near him, the season's last guavas loomed from amidst the moonlit leaves. One, two, three of them . . . so ripe, so heavy, the slightest touch could make them fall from the tree.

He picked one. Perfect Buddha shape. Mulling on its insides, unconcerned with the world . . . Beautiful, distant fruit, growing softer as the days went by, as the nights passed on; beautiful fruit filled with an undiscovered constellation of young stars.

He held it in his hand. It was cool, uneven to his touch. The hours passed. More stars than sky. He sat unmoving in this hushed night.

In the van the Hungry Hop boy was growing more hysterical as he drove. What did he want? He wanted to meet Pinky just as they had planned. No. What he wanted was to turn around and go back to his comfortable bed. Then he wanted to wake up and go downstairs for his morning parathas, cooked just he way he liked them. No. What was he thinking? He remembered all of his sisters and aunties waiting for him. In fact, it never happened that he was allowed to eat even his breakfast in peace.

Pinky saw the van appear around the bend in the road that curved down the hillside below her and picked up the bundle of belongings she had brought with her: 'At last!' But then, mysteriously, she saw the van turn on to an unpaved farm road and disappear again. She couldn't have imagined it, could she? From lack of sleep? But that wasn't like her at all. It must be that fool of a boy. Would she really be able to stand him after all? Well, she would give him a beating with her stick. Just then, the van reappeared. Once more she picked up her bundle. And then . . .

What!

It made a neat beetle-like turn and disappeared again!

*

'To hell with that bloody van,' yelled the Brigadier. Surely this could not be happening? But again and again, driving sometimes in front of them or sometimes behind, disappearing into side streets, then reappearing, was the ice-cream van! 'I am going to shoot him,' the Brigadier vowed, speaking quietly all of a sudden. 'I tell you, I am going to shoot that lunatic dead.'

'Aiii, sir,' said Mr Gupta, sitting up and squawking like an alarmed bird. 'Don't do that, sir. He is only a ice-cream vendor.'

White-faced, the DC hung on to the side of the jeep. What were things coming to? He was caught up in a nightmare. He wasn't even awake and this was a grisly awful nightmare.

Mr Chawla went to check on Sampath. 'They will be here soon,' he said and went back along the path to rejoin Ammaji, who was awaiting the police superintendent at the entrance to the orchard, along with all the roadblock policemen. But the police superintendent was still in bed. For he had decided the night before, in the hope that he might be demoted, to absent himself from this sensitive operation. Happily, with his blanket pulled over his head, he dreamt and snored.

For a minute, the orchard was empty. 'Aha!' thought the spy, still hiding in the bush where Kulfi had passed him a little while ago. The cooking pot stood bubbling enticingly as he darted out towards it and, his heart in his mouth, he clambered up the tree beneath which the pot stood. He would position himself above the cauldron so that he might watch exactly what was going on. In his pocket was his collection of vials and string; hopefully, he would be able to take samples from the gravy while seated above it . . . A man possessed, he edged his way along the branches.

The langurs moved restlessly as morning dawned. The army crawled up the bazaar road. In the back of the Brigadier's jeep lay the Hungry Hop boy, trussed up with monkey nets, firmly tied to keep him from making any more trouble down one way streets. 'Let me go,' he had cried, struggling. 'Let me go. Today I have to decide my life.'

'You are not deciding anything,' the Brigadier had replied. With a scarf taken from Mr Gupta, he tied up the Hungry Hop boy's mouth.

And the Hungry Hop boy fidgeted and struggled in silence, borne towards Pinky despite his vacillations.

'There they are, Sampath,' shouted Mr Chawla when he caught sight of them. 'Sampath! They are here!'

All of a sudden, with explosive alarm, like a physical expression of an exclamation mark, the langurs leapt out of Sampath's tree, confusion and terror upon their faces.

'Keep to the plan,' said the Brigadier. 'Get set . . . Ready . . . Go!'

Clearly, the langurs were wide awake and likely to escape at any moment. The men leapt into battle formation.

'What about the nets, you donkeys? You're supposed to have the nets with you,' yelled the Brigadier.

They should have been unloaded already. But the nets that were to hold the langurs now held the Hungry Hop boy instead and when the soldiers went to get them, they found their efforts to pull them out of the jeep greatly disrupted by his being entangled in them.

Pinky, hearing the noise, arrived to discover that Hungry Hop had been caught by the army. She looked at him with disgust. Oh, the sorry slug. All trussed up like that! She had never appeared so lovely to him, so angry and scornful. Hungry Hop gave her a pleading look, but the expression on her face was unforgiving. He had let her down at a crucial time.

Mr Chawla ran to Sampath's tree to bring him down. He should really have been made to descend earlier. It was already getting dangerous. But . . . wait a minute –

'Sampath,' he shouted. 'Sampath, Sampath, Sampath . . .'

The tree was empty.

'Sampath.' Mr Chawla's voice rose to a shriek that echoed about the hillside and he clutched at his heart. His worst fears had come true. 'Sampath,' he wailed. 'Sampath, where are you? Where are you?'

Ammaji ran to the guava tree, as over her head the monkeys leapt back into it. Its branches moved like the sea with the slam of froth and rough green water. The monkeys jabbered and muttered, widened and narrowed and rubbed their eyes.

'Baba,' wept Miss Jyotsna, who had just arrived to witness this terrible event. She staggered as if she were about to faint – and was caught by Mr Gupta's waiting arms. 'Baba, Baba . . .'

They looked here. They looked there. Up and down the guava tree. In the neighbouring trees. In the bushes. Behind the rocks. They stared up into the branches again and again, into the undisturbed composition of leaves and fruit bobbing up and down. Its painfully empty cot. But wait! Upon the cot lay a guava, a single guava that was much, much bigger than the others: rounder, star-based, weathered . . . It was surrounded by the silver langurs, who stared at it with their intent charcoal faces. On one side was a brown mark, rather like a birthmark . . .

'Wait,' shrieked Ammaji. 'Give me that fruit. Wait! Sampath! Sampath!'

But the Cinema Monkey picked up the fruit himself before anybody had time to move and, calm-eyed and wise, holding it close to his chest, with the other monkeys following in a band, he leapt from the guava tree's branches and bounded away.

'Wait!'

The army chased them, giving up their struggle with the nets. Mr Chawla chased them and Ammaji. The crowd of devotees, who had by now broken through the police lines, and finally even the lazy policemen without their superintendent – how they all ran, wheezing, panting, desperate. Pinky too had joined in the chase. In front of her the Brigadier cut a dashing figure. She was filled with an urge to tweak his buttocks. Hadn't her father told her to set her sights higher than herself, not lower?

The spy crawled farther along the branches and the sound of a rising tempest filled the air as the monkeys jumped over the wall into the university research forest, the tree tops churning as if a whirlwind were passing through, the monkeys' path into the mountains traced by a silver trembling through the pines, by a shivering of branches and foliage. The forest birds flew up and scattered in alarm, their cries mingling with the voices down below, the air full of red and blue and black satin, the golden and brass feathers of pheasants and peacocks, woodpeckers and bulbuls . . .

Still, the monkeys travelled. Higher and higher. Like a gust of wind that comes out of nowhere, rustles through the trees and melts into nothing like a ghost. The crowd stood panting in the orchard. The spy crawled along the branches.

High in a mossy magnolia, gathering orchids, Kulfi was caught up for an instant in a shaking storm, saw a pale blur flash past her. She stood up on the branch where she had been sitting, shielding her eyes against the rays of the sun, to watch as the monkeys climbed on. Up into the wilderness, up to the shoulder of the highest mountain. Here the trees at the very summit wavered for a moment, bowed their heads as if in farewell – and then they were gone. Without a trace.

The air was suddenly still. The birds flew back into the forest. The feathers floated gently down after them.

And in this sudden stillness, from the direction of the orchard, people heard:

A crack!

A howl!

A watery splash!

The sound reached Kulfi in her tree. She turned back down towards the valley. 'What was that?'

'Did you hear?' Pinky fired at the Brigadier with her beautiful big eyes. 'Did you hear that sound?'

'What was that?' asked Mr Chawla and Ammaji, the army men and the policemen, the devotees and the townspeople.

Despite themselves, they drew their attention from the mountain top. Above Kulfi's enormous cooking pot hung a broken branch. In the pot were spices and seasonings, herbs and fruit, a delicious gravy.

And something else.

Gingerly, they approached the bubbling cauldron.